POTOMAC review

Editor-in-Chief
JULIE WAKEMAN-LINN

Poetry Editor
KATHERINE SMITH

Technology Editor
J. HOWARD

Community Outreach Editor
ROBERT GIRON

Administrative Assistant/Webmaster
OM RUSTEN

Associate Editors

ZACHARY BENAVIDEZ	MIKE MAGGIO
STEPHEN BESS	IAN SYDNEY MARCH
DIANE BOSSER	SEAN MORAN
GENEVIEVE CARMINATI	SHANNON O'NEILL
JEANNE MORGAN CASHIN	JULIE PLATT
KATHERINE DAVIS	WARREN REED
SWIFT DICKISON	LEIGH RIDDICK
LISA FRIEDMAN	MICHAEL RYAN
KAROLINA GAJDECZKA	JESSIE SIEGEL
DORY HOFFMAN	JARVIS SLACKS
ALISHA HOROWITZ	LYNN STEARNS
MICHAEL LANDWEBER	MARIANNE SZLYK
KATEEMA LEE	SAMANTHA VENERUSO
MICHAEL LEBLANC	JOHN WANG
LISA LISTER	EDYTHE WISE
DAVID LOTT	HANANAH ZAHEER

Interns
BRIAN APARICIO
MALLORY LINDENBAUM
NOELLE ROYER

Published by the Paul Peck Humanities Institute
at Montgomery College, Rockville, Maryland

The Potomac Review has been made possible through the generosity
of the Montgomery College Foundation.
A special thanks to Dean Carolyn Terry.

Paul Peck Humanities Institute
51 Mannakee Street, Rockville, MD 20850
Copyright 2014

For submission guidelines and more information:
http://www.montgomerycollege.edu/potomacreview

Potomac Review, Inc., a not-for-profit 501 c(3) corp.
Member, Council of Literary Magazines & Presses
Indexed by the American Humanities Index
ISBN: 978-0-9889493-3-1

Subscribe to *Potomac Review*
One year at $20 (2 issues)
Two years at $34 (4 issues)
Sample copy order $12 (Single issue)

Cover Photography by Kathleen Gunton
Front cover photo, "Taking the First Step"
Back cover photo, "Wild Grasses"

Table of Contents

Author	Title	Type	Page
Ned Balbo	From an Exile in Auden's Time	Poem	1
Destiny Birdsong	Emperor of Brown	Poem	2
Jude Brancheau	A History of Hands	Poem	3
Janet Buttenwieser	Chief Complaint	NonFiction	4
Joseph Cassara	Eurydice	Fiction	10
Noel Crook	Reading Ovid at Buzzard Rocks	Poem	15
Holly Day	The Last Day / The Other Woman	Poems	17-18
George Dila	Samson, Brandon, and Me	NonFiction	19
Kaitlin Dyer	If We are to Leave, Let's Leave Together	Poem	29
Nausheen Eusuf	Laundry Hamper	Poem	30
Kristin N. Faatz	In Flight	Fiction	32
Corey Ginsberg	An Encounter with the Bottom of my Womanhood	Poem	36
Eileen Gonzalez	The Book of Jodie	Fiction	37
David Goodrich	Small Hours on the High Plains	NonFiction	43
Paul Grams	Against Penetration / Must We Wait on Later to See the Right?	Poems	49-50
Jeff Hardin	Old Man with a Cane / To Begin / As Much or As Little / What the River Says	Poems	51-56
Peleg Held	Estuary	Poem	57
Ryan Hibbett	Lines for Possum	Poem	58
Amy Holman	The Exact Heart of Mesopotamia	Poem	60
Jane Hoogestraat	A Common Land	Poem	61
Beth Konkoski	A Drawn and Papered Heart	Fiction	62

Rachel Kubie	The Bodies in the Bridges	Poem	69
Gerry LaFemina	Arithmetic	Poem	70
Martin H. Levinson	A Mammoth Lamentation	Poem	71
Peter Makuck	Names	Poem	72
William Miller	Hardy's Soldier/The Bottle Tree	Poems	74-77
Dan Moreau	Everything You Ever Wanted	Fiction	78
Kathleen O'Toole	Sustenance/ Twilight, Ardgroom	Poems	89-93
Eric Reymond	Everything Is Breath	Poem	94
Paige Riehl	Summons	Poem	96
Jane Satterfield	Inheritance/Off-Hand Elegy	Poem	97-99
Mikhail Scherbakov	Returning from a journey, to what I'd long abandoned… translated by Ekaterina Chapiro	Poem	100-101
Wendy Scott	History of Ornament	poem	102
Peter Serchuk	A Day Trip to Ellis Island	Poem	103
Leona Sevick	Any dog will bite/Zoonosis	Poems	104-107
Spencer Smith	Incisor	Poem	108
Peter P. Sordillo	Classical Electrodynamics	Poem	109
Dario Sulzman	Father Frequencies	Poem	110
Kelly M. Sylvester	Adamless Eden	Poem	112
Savannah Thorne	Hurricane Isabel September 12/ Hurricane Isabel September 19/ Hurricane Isabel September 21	Poems	113-115
Tina Tocco	21 Days/Promised Land	Fiction	116-117
LaToya Watkins	Girl	Fiction	118
Colleen Wells	Between Two Poles	NonFiction	126
Kathleen Wheaton	Call It a Night	Fiction	130

From an Exile in Auden's Time
Ned Balbo

Beyond the vacant -isms of the day
that you resist in any age or era
lies a wilderness where what you say
is wrong—dead-wrong—and must be met with Power,

silenced, or conjoined to some idea
that discredits you with all the error
of its shameful practice. Mercy's shown
only when you're irrelevant, or gone,

or willing to concede, when duly pressed,
what you believe you saw you never witnessed.
Power is good and acts with Good in mind—
the larger, public good. Its face is kind,

suffused with light and clarity of vision,
resolved to impose freely, without restraint,
its willful, absolute Imagination
toward a better world. Because you can't.

Give in: survival's better than salvation.
Your conscience isn't clear; nobody's is.
Unwelcome truths will only sow division....
To say more would be pointless, perilous.

Emperor of Brown
Destiny Birdsong

Here's what I love about you:
Brown skin stretched over
Body, stretched over
Bone.
And it is not caramel,
Cocoa,
Or Crayon-colored;
Café au lait,
Pecan tan,
Peanut-butter,
Or any of the names
We typically use.

I think it must be
The color the sun made
When it shone on
Washed-off dirt
For the first time.
While the big-eyed blues
Of sky and sea
Stood aloof
(no longer brilliant,
now insignificant),
There was a moment
Before moments,
Before days
When God said "Let there be
Something."
And the sun?
The sun took the suggestion.
Just took it.
Took it and ran.

A History of Hands
Jude Brancheau

Though they fumbled keys and
strings, they blindly played the simple
climax, the sharps and flats down
unfamiliar backs.
                They hit the curve,
held on to the spiral, the rod and the reel,
the hook and hard lip.
                They angled
my couch, a big table alone, hugged them down
many flights and maneuvered the most
awkward words.
                They helped my kids feel through
their sleeves, slowly turned fairy tales, made
shadow wings on the wall and proved away
the bogeyman.
                They knew *As I Lay*,
the Our Father and the half prayer
of holding another woman's hand.

Chief Complaint

Janet Buttenwieser

When the ambulance came for me, its interior was lined with paper skeletons. They dangled above me like a macabre army, keeping watch as I lay on the gurney. Thick black straps formed an X extending out from each corner of the stretcher, tethering it to the ambulance hull. Thinner straps pinned me to the mattress, one across my legs, the other across my chest. I rested my hands against my hips, nervously plucking at my baggy cotton sweatpants. I wore thick tan socks with blue bears printed on them, and no shoes. Strands of unwashed hair lay across my face and I brushed them away carefully, minimizing movement. My boyfriend, Matt, sat next to one paramedic in the front seat. The other paramedic sat at my right shoulder, a full array of medical instruments and equipment within arms' length. I was the centerpiece of our tableau, and in the center of me, the reason we were all here: a gaping hole in my abdomen where my surgical wound had opened. I had not seen the hole, and though I pictured it as small, I felt no reassurance from this fact. I imagined the worst case scenario: a trip back to the operating table that held my body just two weeks before.

But we weren't talking about the hole. We were talking about traffic. The freeway was unusually jammed for a Saturday morning, and it would be an agonizing crawl to get to the hospital where I'd had surgery.

Matt asked if they could turn on the sirens. "We're only allowed to do that in life-or-death scenarios," the driver replied. Which mine, apparently, was not. It was up to me, the paramedic in the back said, but he would recommend that we go to the university hospital since it was closest to our house. For a moment we were just four people in a car, discussing this as though debating which restaurant to dine at. It's your birthday, Janet. You decide.

The last six months had been full of decisions, ones a healthy twenty-eight-year-old shouldn't have to make. But I was not healthy. At the age of twenty-six, I'd been diagnosed with Crohn's Disease, at the very hospital we were now driving towards. There I'd had the trinity of invasive medical procedures: The Scope, The Probe, The Swallow. I inserted suppositories in solid and liquid form, special-ordered by the pharmacist who came to know me by name. I ingested countless pills – horse-sized tan ones and tiny white ones. It was the tiny ones, Prednisone, that kept me free of symptoms and abloom in side effects: acne, weight gain, headaches. My cheeks swelled to the point that my eyes almost disappeared. I looked like Violet Beauregarde in Charlie and the Chocolate Factory, inflating into a giant blueberry.

Through the ambulance's high windows I caught glimpses of maple tree branches, yellow and orange leaves fluttering against a pale blue background. I imagined the people in the cars around us going to soccer games, to buy last-minute costumes for their kids to wear on Halloween the following evening. Heading out of town to go hiking, apple picking. I pictured all of these people talking, laughing, adjusting their car radios. Oblivious to the ambulance beside them, the pain and suffering within. I had to decide where to go. I closed my eyes.
"University."

My gastroenterologist had been delighted with my response to the Prednisone, the way it kept my symptoms at bay. She was unconcerned about my side effects; I found them worse than the disease itself. I gained twenty pounds. Fifteen of them sat on top of my neck, balloons inflated in each cheek and under my chin. Moon face, the prescription insert called the swelling. Doesn't it sound like a person newly in love, so full of joy they cannot stop smiling? It's not. If I bumped into friends I hadn't seen in awhile, they would look at me with a mixture of horror and confusion.

"Are you taking medication that makes your face swell?" one blunt friend asked across a crowd of people. I went on this way for a year: puffed up, unhappy, swallowing pill after pill.

And then a miracle happened. I went to see a different doctor, who offered a new theory: I did not have Crohn's Disease. The problem, he posited, was on the outside of my intestine. He referred me to a surgeon, one who'd operated on his wife. The surgeon fit the stereotype: tall, athletic, cocky. When I met with him, he sounded excited at the prospect of cutting me open to find out what was inside: a tumor, nestled between my colon and my tailbone.

"It was like a piece of cement in there," the surgeon told me as he removed my staples, all forty of them plinking into a metal bowl while he talked, animated. He was proud of the successful surgery, and we were all relieved at the pathology report sent earlier that week: the tumor was benign. I winced, partly from the pain of the staple removal, and partly from his description of the surgery. I envisioned him with a small jackhammer, chipping the tumor away.

There were two pin-sized holes halfway down my eight-inch incision, just below my navel. Drops of clear fluid occasionally oozed out.

"We see this all the time," the nurse said, taping a piece of gauze over the area. "They'll heal up on their own."

The holes had different ambitions. Getting up from the couch the next morning, I performed the steps they taught me at the hospital: roll to my side, push up to a sitting position. I stood slowly, and midway up, I felt a sharp tug on my belly, as though I were a marionette whose string had been pulled the wrong direction. I sat back down, and called Matt in from the kitchen. He lifted my shirt and peeked under the gauze.

"Okay," he said slowly. "Your wound has opened up a little. Stay right there." He backed into the other room, out of earshot, and called 911.

"Yup," the paramedic said after he arrived and looked under the gauze. "We need to take you to the hospital." Everyone colluded to keep me calm. I did not look at the hole until a week later, with the aid of a mirror. It was far worse than I'd pictured, a valley in the middle of my abdomen. The curled flesh on either side of the hole faced skyward, as though someone were trying to turn my belly inside out.

In the ambulance, the paramedic spoke into the two-way radio. "Twenty-eight year-old female patient complains of dehiscence." He'd taught me this word only moments earlier, the term for a wound opening up. He gave the dispatch nurse my vitals, and signed off.

"Why did you have to say that?" I asked after he hung up, like we were lovers having a quarrel. "I'm not complaining. It's a fact." I applied the same energy to being a patient I'd given to being a student or having a job. I did everything the doctors told me to. I cracked jokes with the nurses. I took my medicine, performed my exercises. I was a perfect patient. The paramedic laughed.

"It's just the term we use. It even says it on the form the doctors fill out. Chief complaint."

Ten years later, I still prickle when I recall the paramedic's words. Actually, it's stronger than a prickling. I feel angry at the way we patients are portrayed by the medical establishment as whiny toddlers who need a nap. Patient complains of gunshot wound to the head. Patient complains of missing limb following leg amputation. Patient would complain of lung collapse, if patient could breathe. When we arrive at the emergency room or the doctor's office, we are not defendants appearing before a judge, whose symptoms are alleged until they can be proven by the doctor beyond a reasonable doubt. We are broken, and we need to tell someone about it so he or she can fix us. We aren't complaining. We are informing. And after all, it is us, not the doctors, who are the experts on our own bodies. They may know how to heal us, but only after we explain to them what is wrong. Maybe that should be the terminology: Patient explains. Patient informs. Wise and talented patient enlightens.

But maybe I have it all wrong. Maybe the actual problem was that I didn't complain enough. A misdiagnosis. A year spent on medication that did terrible things to my body. Countless unnecessary drugs and medical procedures. Hours and hours of time spent in doctors' offices, waiting rooms, procedure rooms. And then my wound tore open. I should have complained, loudly and often. But I was silent, stoic. I communicated my feelings to my family and friends, but brought few of these emotions to my doctors' attentions. If it weren't for a family friend, a doctor, urging me to get a second opinion, who knows where I would be? Probably sitting in the clinic, being treated for a disease I did not have.

After wheeling my gurney into the ER admitting area, the paramedics handed me off to the triage nurse.

"Patient is conscious and alert," my backseat paramedic said, smiling at me as he handed the nurse his clipboard. She signed the papers and handed it back before wheeling me into an exam room. I would not have to go back into surgery, the doctor informed Matt and me, to our great relief. The nurse explained how we would pack the opening with gauze daily until the tissue knitted itself back together. When I asked the nurse why this might have happened, her response was simple.

"Prednisone."

Its effects still lingered, even though I'd taken my last dose over a month before. Prednisone's main purpose is to suppress inflammation, clearing the lungs of people in respiratory distress, or, in my case, relieving the pressure of the growth on my intestine. But inflammation is the body's natural response to healing. With the Prednisone still in my system, my abdomen couldn't join itself back together. Thus, the tear. Perhaps they needed to amend the prescription insert of possible side effects: Weight gain. Acne. Moon face. Flesh-ripping.

"We hate Prednisone," Matt said to the nurse. That was all the complaining I had the energy for, given voice by my boyfriend. I needed only the smallest validation from the nurse. She nodded at Matt, and then turned to look at me. She gave me a small smile.

"I hate it, too."

Eurydice

Joseph Cassara

    It's been months since I've seen my wife. At first she returned every day. Then the days became fewer and the intervals longer. The alcove in my chest has been calcifying for a decade now without her. She was, as Carl would say, summoned back down to the depths yonder. Each night, I play her antique phonograph and sing the saddest songs man has ever heard.
    On Sunday evening she appears in the dining room. She looks like a porcelain doll wrapped in silk damask. I say, Eurydice, don't you know it's God's day.
    She says, Well it's my day now.
    I didn't think you'd come, I say.
    Whenever I see her, I feel like the tallest man on Earth. She wears her wedding dress each time and I ask if we can dance again. She says no and I ask why.
    You asked me last time, and the time before, she says.
    But I just want to touch you, I say.
    We can't touch, she says. There are rules.
    Okay, I say, then hold out your hand so I can see it.
    She reaches out her hand and I turn on the lamp.
    Eurydice? I say. Can I look at you?
    Yes, she says and I'm silent. From the side, in that dress she wore pregnant on our wedding day, she looks like an ampersand. I look at her palm, soft and gray, the color of winter sand. I look at her face, iridescent like a moth wing, lines mark her age. I look at her eyes and she looks back.
    Wait here, I say.
    I turn my back and go into the bedroom, place the step stool in front of the closet, and reach for my old tuxedo on the

last hanger. I shed my old clothes like dead skin and leave them on the floor. I squeeze into the tux and walk back down the hallway and into the dining room. She is standing in the lamp light.

Can we dance now? I ask. Look, I'm wearing my tux for you.

She sighs. Orpheus, she says. You can't touch me, that was the rule.

We used to be, as the town folk say, circus freaks. We learned to love that term, and the hardest kind of love is the kind you need to learn. We used to dance for the crowds, traveling the country, sometimes the world, she and I and the rest of us.

Our names were painted in globs on a piece of plywood—Orpheus & Eurydice: The Smallest Couple in the World. The crowds would gather: men in round hats and bow ties, women in dresses, children held together with suspenders and trousers, each taller than the next. Cameras popped their flashes, and the film captured us frozen.

Their faces: first, contorted in curiosity.

(Who is this couple and why are they so small?)

We would sway together, palm against palm, to the sound of an accordion, like jewel box ballerinas.

Their faces: then, gentle recognition.

(They are in love.)

Her skin felt so smooth against mine. We swayed as if we were jointless, boneless, and all soul.

Their faces: finally, detachment.

(We have seen enough of this. Where are the candy apples?)

We would spin individually, parting under their gaze, only to return back again, palm against palm, as they walked away in search of their apples.

Can you at least spin for me? I ask.

She spins and the lamp light hits the silk. The tip of her dress lifts off the floor and I see her toes.

You look twenty again, I say.

Outside the wind scratches the tree branches against the building. We stand in the middle of the room near the table. I smell the vanilla from her perfume.

Can you even recognize me anymore? I ask. I must look so old to you.

Didn't you go to church today? she says.

No, I say, I've stopped going. The children are scared of me. I make the young ones cry.

Oh don't say that, Orpheus.

They do. It's true. They look at me with such horror, like I'm the ugliest thing.

They're just young, she says. They don't know any better.

Somewhere outside, the bird that has been singing all day goes mute. I didn't realize it had been singing until the singing stopped.

They've always looked at us that way, she says. So what?

I'm getting old and I'm tired of seeing that look in their eyes. I have to deal with it alone.

She looks at me and I remember the day she lost the baby. The war had just ended and people were looking for magic. There were sharp pains, blood.

Back then, Carl was the ringmaster. She went into labor, but there was no crying. And we knew. That night, even the stars felt frozen.

Carl set up a special side tent for Eurydice and me. The show had to go on. She bottled her pain, and I held her close to me as we spun for the crowd. Watch as they dance, Carl boomed from his soapbox, watch as the magic happens, watch her and watch her and watch.

Now, I watch her gaze as she stares into me. Her eyes are clear marbles, and she asks, How is Brunhilde?

She shaved her beard, I say.

No! she says. When? Did she cry?

Some weeks ago, I say. She didn't cry, she just looked so tired under all that hair. We'll have to shut down soon. No one believes anymore. The elephants are dying. People have computers now.

All of the elephants? she asks. What is a computer?

Only some of them, I say. It's a device that's hard to explain. It has a screen and a memory, it can talk and hear, but it has no emotions.

Oh, she says. Sounds scary.

There are worse things, I say.

Silence.

And Wotan? she says. How is he?

A bit arthritic, but he still walks the tightrope.

That man will die on the tightrope, she says.

I feel like there's so much I wanted to ask you, I say. But I can't remember.

So ask me next time, she says.

When is next time? I ask.

I don't know, she says. Soon. You should keep a notebook of things to say to me, so you won't forget.

She glides over to the lamp and looks at my grandmother's old mirror leaning against the wall.

You didn't cover it, she says.

Was I supposed to?

Oh Orpheus, you always forget.

She stands in front of the mirror. I'm behind her, looking over her shoulder. She looks at herself and her eyebrows arch down. She reaches her hand towards the glass.

I can't see myself, she tells the mirror.

But I can see you, I tell her.

I don't like what I see, though I don't tell her that. The Eurydice in the mirror looks older, sicker. The skin on her neck cracks like a sugar cookie, her thinning hair is damp seaweed. I don't want to remember her that way. Her last years.

Orpheus, stop crying, she says.

I'm not, I say.

I can feel her silence in my fingernails.

There is no such thing, she says, as forever.

[What god do I need to pray to, I think, and what is Her name?]

Dance with me, I say. Please.

You already know that if you touch me, I'll never be able to come back.

Eurydice, look at me. I'm an old man. It's been years since I've felt you.

I walk over to the lamp and untwist the bulb.

That's not how this works, she says. There are certain rules.

The rules, the rules, I say, the rules. I didn't know there were any rules.

That's what you said the first time.

We stand in the middle of the dining room as the bird begins to sing once more. I see my reflection in the mirror. The bird song is the most beautiful song I have ever heard, and when I touch her, she is gone.

There is a fallen puddle of silk on the floor and I'm standing in my tuxedo and the clock on the wall is broken and I say Eurydice where are you and I say Eurydice but I'm not sure if the words carry any sound.

Reading Ovid at Buzzard Rocks
Noel Crook

April, and I've come back to this blunt horizon
butting up against a bell jar of blue
and a sun that can bake the meat off anything,

even loss. Where if you hold out your arms
at the bluff's edge and breathe deeply enough,
the sky will agree

to swallow you whole. But it's turkey mating season
again, the lovelorn, dusty hens congregating
over on Horse Hill, scooting willy-nilly in

and out of sage and prickly pear, addled
by their need, and the water
I cool my feet in is the same

pale cataract that once spilled
past me as a girl when I sunbathed
on the dam, dreaming of the boy I'd kissed

at summer camp, whose mouth drowned out
Led Zeppelin's "Stairway to Heaven,"
his breath on my neck, the way my heart let go

its dry tap-dance, floundered like a downed
bird, the weight of his hands like ballast on my hips—
and the hens scatter and drift haphazard as ash,

waiting for kettle-drum calls of the gobblers
roosting solitary and oily in the cottonwoods,
their bristled beards swinging

like scalp belts. After this long coyote winter,
all of us still wanting to be stitched
into the old cloth of the world's desire,

still wading these shallow waters, traipsing
these same parched hills, waiting for the sudden
shadow blocking out the sun, the beating

of wings, something, anything, to pin us down
under all this blue sky.

The Last Day
Holly Day

I hid the baby beneath the floorboards, prayed
for his quiet. I stretched out over the spot, covered his hiding
    place
with my body, whispered to my son through the rough timbers
don't cry. please don't cry.

footsteps rattled past the door, and I covered
my head with a pillow, my body
with a quilt. if anyone looked in through the door or the window
they'd just see a messy room. if they came into the house
they'd see me.

night came, and I could smell smoke seep into the house
could hear people running, screaming past the window
gunshots and heavy machinery. I pulled the sleeping baby
out of the hole in the floor, woke him to nurse
prayed for rain.

The Other Woman

Holly Day

(dim the lights a little more, gather your belongings
leave. Fling a crimson rag on top of the bare bulb
next to the divan—wheel in the post-holocaust gag city mock-up
and permit the vermin to commence loping through the maze.)
I'm walking in your ideas, in a colorless seaside scene, naked
    feet
leaving no footprints in the sand. This chunk of ass

is the single solitary genuine human being here tonight. Wings
of seraph hammer against the glass windows of the inn, insensitive
to everything excluding our blind sins. (pour a couple additional
pails of murder on the coastline, wrap up the distended cadavers,
destroy the rats). I nearly telephoned you yet again last night,
imagining that the phone was right by your head, but I knew

that disgusting thing would be staying over for the weekend
and would pick up the phone, stockpiling your calls—I
enfolded the pink, synthetic die-cast receiver between my
    sodden thighs
and imagined I was hoarding sections of you through these
    hallucinations.
(the Armageddon recreation will go back to the beginning by
    itself
tomorrow. Let's call it a day. The conclusion of any epoch signifies

something has to die.)

Samson, Brandon and Me
George Dila

In a vintage family photo album there is a snapshot of me at the age of two or so, perched atop an ottoman-sized boulder in what appears to be a formal, public garden. I am wearing bibbed short pants and high-top leather shoes, what the well-dressed little boy was wearing in the early 1940s. My dimpled hands rest comfortably at my sides. My face radiates sunny contentment and innocence. But what is most striking about this picture is my hair, a mass of soft, light curls sitting atop my head like a happy little cloud. That is quite likely the best my hair has ever looked.

This simple photograph, glossy black and white with deckle edges, is a minor family treasure, a tiny pictorial anecdote in the Dila family history – little Gee-Gee in curls. The jaded, tetchy man I now am gazes into this tiny face with wonder and disbelief. Could this small, sweet boy have metamorphosed into me? When I show her the picture, my One-True-Love confirms that I was as cute as a whole jarful of buttons, not to mention countless bugs' ears. My older sister verifies this assessment, with a pinch on my cheek. My older brother has not seen the picture in many years, but I can predict his reaction if I were to show it to him now. "Nice hair, bro" he'd say, and hand it back.

What to do with my hair has been an on-going battle, a tonsorial struggle lasting seven decades. Except for those first couple of years, my hair has been bland and lackluster, the color of the dust one finds in sidewalk cracks, and as lifeless as the planet Mars. I have always envied, resented may be an even better word, the robust black shock of the Latino and the Asian, the thick blonde thatch of the Scandinavian. But alas, my hair is disappointing middle-European hair. I have spent a lifetime trying to make it look good.

Other Dila-family pictures document the decades of struggle. A few years after the head of soft curls, another black and white snapshot, taken no doubt with my father's Kodak Brownie, reveals a smooth, slicked-over style accomplished with the help of something from a bottle, oily and scented. There is a knife-sharp part on the left side. This look, as well as what I am wearing, seem to suggest my mother's reluctant acceptance that Gee-Gee had grown out of babyhood into boyhood. I am dressed in a knickers suit of the heaviest, most abrasive wool tweed, knee socks, high-top shoes, a white shirt, and tie, hand-knotted, of course. No cheesy clip-ons for Dila boys. I am about to enter the back seat of our fat, maroon Plymouth. It is Sunday morning. The family is headed for church.

Samson. Now there was a guy with great hair

It was probably around this time, and at that place, that I first heard the story of the Old Testament hero Samson, another man with serious hair issues. Samson exhibited such moral courage, physical strength, and devotion to his God that he led the Jews for twenty years, slaughtered countless Godless Philistines (was there any other kind?), became a legend in three of the world's major religions and, three thousand years later, in a place called America, gave his name to a line of nearly indestructible two-suiters, Pullmans and overnight cases.

In the Baptist Sunday School version of his story, Samson's superhuman strength was a gift from God, his to enjoy as long as he did not cut his hair. We were not told the whole story, of course, which was the case with most of what we were taught in Baptist Sunday School. But that's another story altogether.

Samson had taken a Nazirite vow of complete commitment to Yahweh, which included the admonition against cutting the hair, as well as against imbibing of the fermented grape. Actually, the commitment was made for him by his mother, who was visited by an angel while she was pregnant, but that is yet another story.

Of course, it was the seductress Delilah, herself a Godless Philistine, who coerced Samson into revealing the secret of his strength. Baptist Sunday School did not provide details of how she exacted this information, presumably not water-boarding, but that is still another story. And yet one more story was the Cecil B. DeMille Hollywood version, released in the year of my birth, but that was more about the make-believe screen magic between a lissome Victor Mature and a sublime Hedy Lamarr than it was about ancient Jewish musclemen and Godless Philistine hussies.

When Samson's hair was cut off as he slept on Delilah's bosom, the way I prefer to imagine the event, his Nazirite vow was broken and Yahweh abandoned him.

Biblical scholars speculate that Samson may have been a skinny wimp rather than the oiled-up, Arnold Schwarzenegger type depicted in the many works of art devoted to him; more like the hollow-chested fellow on the beach who gets sand kicked in his face by the bully before he bulks up with the help of Charles Atlas who, by the way, had a pretty healthy head of hair to go along with those bulging biceps and pecs. This theory would explain why the Godless Philistines were always so amazed by Samson's periodic shows of strength. After all, when Samson used his great strength, the sacred text says "the Spirit of the Lord came upon him in power," presumably transforming him from a weakling into, well . . . into Samson. Like The Hulk, only Jewish.

Absalom was another Old Testament hero with hair problems we learned about in Sunday School. King David's fairest and most beloved son was, with his long, flowing tresses, deemed the most beautiful man in the kingdom. But his hair betrayed him, too. On horseback, fleeing the armies of David's general Joab after a failed coup attempt against his father, his locks got caught up in the branches of an oak tree, rendering him as helpless as a piñata, vulnerable to the spears and swords of Joab's men.

The Crew Cuts didn't wear crew cuts

Regrettably, there are no known pictures of Samson or Absalom as boys, but there are plenty of me, one of which was taken on a family camping trip. The whole family is in this picture, so exactly who snapped it shall forever remain a mystery. All of us, mom and dad and the three kids, are busy at tasks. I am on my knees, pretending to hammer a wooden stake into the stony ground to hold a rope attached to one corner of our heavy canvas tent. I can remember the smell of this tent as if it were yesterday, the intense, sweet aroma of oiled canvas billowing out from its core as it was unfolded onto the bare earth after its long winter's nap in the basement. In this photo, I have progressed to the basic crew cut, my fair hair limply hugging the contours of my skull, similar to the way Brandon de Wilde wore his hair in the movie Shane, both Brandon and I on our way to hollow-chested adolescence. Our crew cuts, Brandon's and mine, were nothing like the crew cuts worn by The Crew Cuts pop group at about that time, which, although cut moderately short, were not true crew cuts at all but, rather, a puffed-up Hollywood version. Sh-Boom.

A few years later, his hair now long and full and wavy, the adolescent Brandon lost his screen virginity to the radiantly innocent, adolescent Carol Lynley in the controversial movie Blue Denim, in the process leaving her screen character in a family way. Unlike Brandon, I had no luck with girls at that age, nor did my hair grow full and wavy.

My father was cutting my hair in those days, using manual squeeze-type clippers. It was a monthly ritual of pure torture – of pulled short hairs, raw nape, and maddeningly itchy neck and chest and back caused by microscopic clippings that, as if by evil magic, somehow found their way through the garrote of towel around the throat. The smell of witch hazel lingered for hours.

When I could finally pay for my own haircuts, and therefore choose my own hair style, I followed my big brother into flat-top country, pomaded up with Lucky Tiger Butch Wax. There is a picture, this one in color, of my brother and me in the foyer a fancy restaurant where we were attending a Baptist youth banquet, the two of us posing in mock-formality before an antique console. I'm guessing that I was about 14, he about 17. We both wore suits, white shirts, ties, and polished shoes, the ensembles of our own choosing and care. We each sported a fresh, shiny flat-top.

Soon enough, I grew out of the flat-top, literally, and moved on to a Princeton cut, as close as I would ever get to the Ivy League, my tweedy fantasy. The Princeton was not long enough for a side part, so my barber, Bert, cut a perfect faux-part with his clippers, leaving just enough in front for a soft roll.

Hoodlum hair and leather jackets

Although we were able to have pretty much any haircut we wanted as teenagers, our father drew the line at the square, blunt cut across the back. That was taboo. We had to have the tapered back, the nice-boy look, as opposed to the straight-across hoodlum look, like our pal Sid wore his.

Sid was Armenian, with hair like Eddie Fisher, dark and full, the kind I'd always wanted. Along with the prohibition on the square-back haircut was the ban on the black leather jacket – both the haircut and the leather jacket evidence of lax parenting, and the foreshadowing of delinquency in youth and a dissolute adulthood. Sid wore just such a jacket when he wasn't wearing his gas station coveralls, the dark blue ones with his name stitched in red cursive on a white oval patch above the breast pocket. He put every cent he made as a gas jockey into his '32 Ford roadster hot rod. On the other hand, my brother's first car, which in rare benevolent moods he allowed me to drive, was a dark green 1947 Hudson Hornet four-door, to which neither the word "hot" nor "rod" would apply. Sid's parents, possibly not recognizing the Devil's influence on their son, let him have his hair any damned way he pleased.

My high school senior picture shows me in my Princeton cut, wearing a brown tweed suit I remember well, having chosen and paid for it myself. I had a nice boy's job in a supermarket, not a bad boy's job like gas jockey or, more unsavory yet, pinsetter in a bowling alley, a place where smokers and beer drinkers lurked. I kept this hair style through an unsuccessful year and a half in Ann Arbor, where French 102, Shakespeare, and several other courses now forgotten defeated me in the best two-out-of-three falls, the same margin by which the flamboyant Gorgeous George took the AWA world wrestling title from the more skilled, but regrettably more rule-abiding, Chief Don Eagle. Gorgeous George had the most famous hair in America in the 1950s, more famous even than the voluptuous tresses of Marilyn Monroe, the original blonde bombshell, or the stern, platinum waves of Kim Novak. Imagine – in a decade in which the flattop was the most popular hairstyle for men, Gorgeous George's hair was grown long, dyed blonde, curled, and decorated with gold-plated bobby pins. If I have one life to live, Gorgeous George probably thought, let me live it as a blonde.

Uncle Sam cuts my hair

My academic failures drove me into the welcoming arms of Uncle Sam, who renamed me RA16621348 and shaved me to the scalp. For three years I did not have to worry about what to do with my hair, allowing it to grow to the standard enlisted-man's length, and no further.

During my two-year tour in Germany, no matter how much I tried to disguise myself as a native, driving an old VW Beetle and wearing clothes bought in local stores, my haircut always gave me away. My mother saved pictures I'd sent home, me in places like Cologne, Copenhagen, London, and Paris, wearing narrow pants, a broad-shouldered sports coat, and tapered shoes, what the well-dressed European hipster was wearing fifty years ago, but without the matching Continental mane. Imagine Jean-Paul Belmondo in Breathless with a GI haircut. Would the delicious Jean Seberg have hitched a ride with him to Marseilles? Absolutely not.

Following my Army years, entering the academic ring for the second time to do battle with foreign languages and atomic numbers, then seeking respectable employment, then seeking out and meeting my One-True-Love-to-be, my struggle for hair style fulfillment continued. Our wedding pictures reveal a longer, slightly puffier slicked back style, probably held in place with some now-banned aerosol.

But wait! What's this picture? My One-True-Love and I, dressed completely in clothing we have tie-dyed ourselves, swirls of color, rainbows, explosions of color, posing in front of our own tie-dye booth, Dream Dyes, at a local crafts fair. My hair is now down to my shoulders! Tie-dyed clothing and Samson-length hair – my struggle has come to this.

The decades fly by, more styles, more pictures, my hair is sometimes business length, sometimes violinist length, sometimes blown dry, sometimes gelled into submission. There is even a butch-cut period about twenty years ago, when, every two weeks, my barber simply ran clippers over my whole head with a Number 2 blade-guard, leaving stubble a mere 5mm in length. Following that short-lived experiment, my hair returned to medium length, sometimes swept back, sometimes with a part, sometimes without, sometimes glistening, sometimes bone dry. And all this time, the hairline receding, back, back, inexorably back, and a growing round patch toward the rear thinning to a gauzy cover.

And then, another revolution.

What about tangles?

I said goodbye to Ron, my barber. He touched my hair with neither scissors nor clippers for nearly three years. The tips of my locks reached my shoulders again, as they had forty years before during the tie-dye period. Some mornings I went for the feral look. Other mornings I tried to tame it, with conditioners, or a dab of this, or a spritz of that. Sometimes I pulled it into a ponytail. My friends looked at me strangely, and asked where I was going with this. I'd have told them if I knew.

For insight I visited websites dedicated to long hair for men – there were several, places where one could find hints on hair volume and color, and discuss topics like "What about tangles?" and "Will people think I'm gay?" The answer to that one? No. Long hair for men was in, according to Hollywood, our final arbiter of fashion acceptability. Think of Colin Farrell as Alexander. On second thought, forget Colin Farrell as Alexander. He was gay. Think, rather, of Brad Pitt as Achilles, Vigo Mortensen as Aragon. Long hair was sexy, its proponents claimed. It enhanced your animal magnetism. Chicks dug it. My One-True-Love questioned whether this could be true, and if it was, why it would make any difference to me.

This might have been my last chance to get it right, the style I would stay with forever. One never knows. I wanted people to look at my hair and see a rebel; one who could wear his hair any damned way he pleased. I wanted them to look at my hair and think of Achilles or Aragon; look at my hair and think of

Samson, even Absalom; look at my hair and think of me as anything but the old man I was becoming.

Detente

I am back in my chair at Ron's Barber Shop. Ron is his usual, affable self, treating me as if I'd been seeing him regularly for the past three years, relying on him to keep my hair orderly and presentable.

"Cut if off," I tell him.

He obliges, without comment. Wasting no time, he loosely braids the long back, then takes tight hold of the braid near the nape of my neck and unceremoniously lops off with sharp scissors what it had taken my follicles a few years to grow. There is no mourning the loss, no tearful goodbye. Ron drops the clump of hair to the floor, where it will be joined by most of what's left on my head, then be swept up with a push broom, and tossed out with the trash.

My head feels light. Free. And with each succeeding snip of the scissors, each pass of the clippers, it feels lighter and freer.

"How do you want the sides?" he asks.

Until that question, we haven't discussed hair at all. We've made small talk – the weather, the Lions-Green Bay game. But now it's decision time. I've given up trying to remind people of Achilles or Aragon, or even Absalom. And the happy little cloud that had once sat atop my head is a faded black and white memory. But I don't want to be the old guy, either – the codger for whom the only appropriate style is the nubby old man's cut.

"Not too short," I say. "Leave it a little long on top, too."

Ten minutes later I am out of the chair, peering closely into Ron's wall-sized mirror. I turn this way and that, run my hand along the side of my head, ruffle the top a bit. What color my hair once had has faded, not to a distinctive pearly white, or a distinguished salt and pepper, but to the un-color of chewed gum. It is shocking how quickly it has thinned, how light and feathery it has become.

"Well, I look ten years younger than when I walked in," I tell Ron.

"At least," he says. "At least ten."

"See you in three weeks," I say as I walk out, my quest for hair distinction ended. My hair is what it is, will be what it will be. There are no further options.

But I'm thinking about an earring. Maybe a small gold loop.

If We are to Leave, Let's Leave Together

Kaitlin Dyer

We pass over cities trailing
like spiders. Like electric eels
moving their way. I know
there is no yellow brick to guide us.
We are in this steel bird
and we ask the steward
for a little more apple juice.
Our marriage is like two boys
burning the entire kitchen
without even finding a match.

Laundry Hamper

Nausheen Eusuf

Your dirty laundry is my friend
and confidante. I know them all:
your Victoria's Secrets and your sweats,
your jeans and knits and halter tops.

They are safe here. I lap them up,
each morsel carelessly flung,
still aglow with your body's warmth,
and cherish the scent of you.

It inflames and intoxicates.
And yet I sense what perfumes
and fragrant soaps conceal,
the wordless sorrows of the flesh.

Overhead, your suits and slacks
hang haughtily, neat and pressed
from the drycleaner's, and smirk
at the plebeian brood I nurse.

I lack affectation. I don't pose
or primp or pretend. My dirty pile:
this is real, raw, uncensored.
Entropy, in life as in nature.

Evenings I watch you make dinner,
or read, or laugh, or make love—
while I ache here in the dark
behind the slatted closet door.

What consolation can we find,
what salve for sorrow? When day is done,
I watch you sleep, knowing that
no one has loved you as I have.

In Flight

Kristin N. Faatz

I'm sorry you have to fly coach. It's my fault: by the time I called in to reserve your tickets, they had already sold all the first-class seats. Lately I haven't been organized enough. I have no excuse except the way I've been feeling.

I did get you the aisle seat closest to the rear restrooms. The engines will be loud, but I'll pack your earplugs and CD Walkman in the carryon, along with the wheat husk neck pillow and lavender sleep mask. You should use the mask if you feel stressed. Lavender always helps me relax. You know I keep that bottle of oil on my nightstand for my insomnia. Somehow the scent always slows my pulse down and unknots my stomach. I have a feeling I'll use it more often while you're away – you know I don't like to sleep alone, and these days I have a hard time staying comfortable – but I don't want you to worry. Of course I'll manage fine.

We'll make sure you get to the airport earlier this time. You don't want to run through the terminal in your sockfeet again: they call it "Filthadelphia" for a reason. I know it's a pain to wait so long before boarding, but hopefully this time you won't have three little kids in the seats across from you in the waiting area. You were anxious about your Orlando trip, I know. That was a big opportunity for you, and you wanted to be rested and focused when you arrived for the concert, not to mention all the radio interviews they had scheduled for you beforehand. It certainly didn't help that you had to cram everything into your pockets and sprint from the security check to the gate, though I did drag both carry-ons so you could re-string your belt and lace up your shoes. When we finally got there, out of breath and panicky, you didn't want to be greeted by a shrieking infant or a toddler who couldn't keep his sticky fingers off your new leather briefcase. I can understand that.

Still, you have to admit at least the little girl stayed in her seat, perfectly well-behaved. She looked like she was about five years old, don't you think? I loved watching her play with her My Little Ponies. You probably didn't hear, but she had Fluttershy tell Applejack all about the airport and the people in it and the exciting imaginary places the planes went off to, countries made out of clover and rainbows and all sorts of things. It was wonderful. But my main point is that the poor mother did the best she could with the smaller ones. Toddlers like shiny things, and maybe that little boy just had a fine taste for Italian leather. You didn't need to tell everyone in earshot how people shouldn't travel with small children, and I hope with all my soul that no one but me heard you say, "If they insist on having them."

On the flight, please try to be patient. You know when there's turbulence, you have to stay in your seat with your belt on. Please don't bring out your credentials this time. Of course in Detroit you're irreplaceable, but at thirty thousand feet, your job is no more important than anyone else's. The pilot couldn't conduct your orchestra, certainly, but meanwhile, you can't fly his plane.

You can't get to the restroom when they're bringing the beverage cart through. Please don't start another argument with the flight attendant, because they can't change the rules. I put your antacids and Imodium in the carryon too, but you can help yourself even more if you avoid the candy bars at the newspaper stand. Just one is plenty. You should also stick to cranberry juice or ginger ale on the flight. Please don't spend five dollars on two swallows of vodka; I know I shouldn't harp on this, but we really need to be more careful now.

Something else: please don't stay in the restroom any longer than you have to. I shouldn't bring it up again, but you didn't absolutely have to change into your tuxedo on the flight to Orlando. We weren't that far behind schedule. I'm sure nobody appreciated the wait while you changed, but most of all, I felt terrible about that mother and her three kids. You didn't realize at the time, I'm sure, but they were sitting right in front of the restroom and they had to listen to all of your banging around. Your language seemed excessive even if you did drop a cufflink into the toilet. I know the kids weren't old enough to understand the words they heard, but the little girl's eyes got so big at all the thumping and shouting. I wanted to hug her and tell her everything was all right, especially because her poor mother had her hands full with the baby in her lap and the toddler who wouldn't stay in his seat, but of course parents don't want total strangers hugging their children. Kids get scared when adults are impatient and yelling. Please, now and in the future, try to remember that.

For the next trip, we might want to replace your carryon. I know you don't want to put your music in your checked luggage, but everyone needs space in the compartments and your suitcase is a bit oversized. Next time we'll have even more to carry. Maybe we could find something smaller that will still hold your music and CDs and hair tonic and cologne and so forth, or if you want to keep this suitcase, you could fit some of my things in it. Then I can use my carry-on for…all the extra things.

I wish I could come with you this time. You know I don't want to miss your concert, but I don't want to be the one hogging the plane's restroom, and you don't need a sick wife hanging on you in Detroit when you'll be so busy. Plus, nobody needs to see the Maestro's wife all bloated and swollen out of shape the way I am.

You know I'll be thinking about you. Watching you is the best part of any concert. Do you remember the first time I saw you? Nothing could have prepared me for that evening, even though I had heard so much about the new young conductor at the symphony. I had never seen such force and grace combined in one person, or known that one pair of hands – your hands, your fingers holding the baton – could be so powerful and yet so tender. I had never seen anyone become such a perfect conduit for music. That night, I couldn't tell where you ended and the music began. Neither of you could have existed without the other.

Why should you have noticed me, out of all those people who came to congratulate you after that concert? I am not brilliant or beautiful or extraordinary in any way. I have no illusions about that.

Tomorrow night and the next nights after, I will sit here at home and work on the blanket I'm knitting and think about you there onstage in Detroit with your musicians, looking the way you did when you took my breath away. Even on the night of the performance, with the white lights beating down and the players spread out before you and the audience behind, I know you'll feel me here waiting. Both of us.

When you fly home, I'll wait at the gate. If there's a group, you'll see me right in front.

Remember us, love. We need you here.

An Encounter with the Bottom of my Womanhood
Corey Ginsberg

A quiet drama, this collapse of infrastructure.
Sheet of paper plummeting onto stack of paper. Not quite
a book but enough flat layers to provide
a jumping-off point.

Of course it's dark here. Gut dark, black soot
nook so far removed from saturation
it can't conceive of a better way to facilitate.
An echo from within reclaims each primal drive.

Behold the bottom: a complete set, a folded
full house, a raw depravity. Maybe amid the ruins
there's a penumbra, a squinted hint, a throat-
clearing warble of realism. Or only this calm flat.

The bottom is a place, like any other. Except
from here everything appears
to have big shoulders and small hips. A cavernous womb
tomb that allows the wanting out of wants.

An underlying assumption: there's a top.
Or at least a scream that reverberates, an unhinging
of vocals offered again and again, until posture assumes
the body is better off hollow.

The Book of Jodie
Eileen Gonzalez

The room tried too hard to look pleasant and unthreatening. Floral-patterned wallpaper blended into the olive carpet without even a baseboard for contrast. The furniture consisted entirely of soft angles and felt like sandpaper. Months-old magazines enticed readers with photos showing The Ascent of Man and Princess Anne's engagement, but I didn't touch them. I reminded myself that I only needed to spend one hour in that place. It didn't help.

I tapped my index finger against my thigh. Dad sat beside me, stiff-backed and neutral. He originally planned to make Mummy drive me here, but I begged him to bring me instead. I could endure anything as long as I knew Dad would be there in the end.

The click of a door exploded in the silence. All I can bring myself to recall about the face of the man who opened it are his horrific smile and even more horrific eyes. They were a vulture's eyes, devoid of all feeling except the readiness to pounce at the slightest hint of wrongdoing. The fact that his idea of wrongdoing differed so violently from my own made my heart twist. I looked to Dad, a plea for mercy.

"You did promise," he said. Well, what was I supposed to say? No?

I dragged my feet through the smiling vulture's doorway. He introduced himself as Dr Lyme, making sure to emphasise how much he cared about my mental health and how helpful he would be if only I allowed it. I twitched as the door shut us in.

I still dream of Lyme's office sometimes, with its stern wooden desk and greying walls and windows far too small to offer comfort. I feel the tacky blue chair through my clothes as I press back into it in a futile attempt to escape that awful, cheerful face, my palms sweating against the armrests. I see the wall behind him boasting framed justifications for his title of psychiatrist. I'd already decided the man didn't deserve this distinction and resolved to call him simply Lyme, at least for the moment. I could think of worse names if he proved half as nasty as he looked.

"Now then." He eyed the papers on his desk. "Joshua, yes? Is that what you like to be called, or is there some other name you prefer?"

I preferred Jodie. I would use it as a stage name when I began my record-shattering musical career. Jimmy always teased me about Jodie being a girls' name, and I hadn't decided on a surname yet, but that didn't stop us from spending our Saturdays singing along to the radio with pencils taped into makeshift microphones, and a mirror borrowed from Mummy's vanity providing instant feedback on our every move.

"Joshua's fine," I said.

"Very well then." He straightened the papers and clicked open his pen. "Let's get straight to business, shall we?"

Straight to business. Never heard that one before. "Let's."

"How long have you had these... fantasies?"

From the moment Jimmy laughed at the word shittim in catechism class. He wasn't subtle about it either: he just shook his copper mane and belted it out, his normally steady sienna eyes shut in mirth. Soon enough, I laughed with him, and when we had to spend the rest of class in opposite corners, I couldn't bring myself to care. Father O'Donnell instructed us to spend our punishment in reverent self-reflection, but I spent it imagining Jimmy as one of my back-up dancers, with a bright silk shirt, white leather trousers and matching waistcoat, and hair just like Brian Connolly's. Mummy fretted when she heard of my misbehaviour, but Dad assured her that such antics were typical of new teenagers and took me to the cellar to help me finish carving my new jewellery box.

I could have told Lyme all of this. I also could have jumped off the Eiffel Tower when my family visited Paris last summer.

"I used to steal my mother's jewellery and put on her make-up when she was out," I said.

"And how long have you fancied other boys?"

I tried and failed to control the shudder. I hated the way he said it, so clinical and formal, like he was describing a condition and not a person. Like my feelings were nothing more than exhibits to be studied and evaluated and fixed.

"That's none of your business."

"I want to help you, Joshua." And I want to be Richard Nixon in front of the Watergate Committee. "I can't do that if you won't talk to me."

"Well, I don't want to answer."

"Alright." He sounded agreeable enough, but I had the impression he would try to squeeze the information out of me later. I needed to stay alert with this one. He'd swindle Pope Paul if given a chance.

"Do you ever feel neglected at home?"

"No. Do you?"

"Are you left alone for long periods? Do your parents pay enough attention to you?"

"Yes. I mean, no. I mean no, they don't leave me alone and yes, they pay me lots of attention!"

My heart and stomach felt like they'd switched places, sending a column of white heat through my ribcage. I knew he would try to make me twist my words into a net he could use to drag me back for future sessions. I just hadn't expected it so soon. I hoped Jimmy's parents wouldn't bring him here. They looked angrier than Mummy when they caught us in the church garden, our lips joined in what we foolishly believed to be an innocent gesture. Only Dad saw it as I did and spent the evening distracting me with stories of his childhood in Ireland as I rubbed my eyes red. I could only hope he would do the same when I escaped this latest example of Mummy's tough love.

Lyme peered at me out of the corners of narrowed eyes, like I was hiding his digital watch behind my back and insisting I wasn't. As if I'd want that new-fangled monstrosity.

"Don't you ever feel neglected at all?" he asked, and I swear I saw the start of another smile curling his thin lips.

"Yeah, but everyone feels that way sometimes. You'd be out of a job if life was perfect."

He laughed a laugh just as ugly as he and said I had a point. Of course I did.

The meeting dragged. Lyme asked stupid questions. I gave stupid answers or none at all. I didn't bother to hide my constant checking of the (non-digital) clock to my right, or my sighs when I realised God hadn't finished testing me. Still, Job's trials were far more challenging than this. I could handle one self-important prat. I only had to zone out Lyme and replay God's words to another Joshua: Have not I commanded thee? Be strong and of a good courage; be not afraid, neither be thou dismayed: for the Lord thy God is with thee whithersoever thou goest....

Oh, I knew He hadn't said it for me. But sometimes, after another week of sitting alone during break or another fight with Mummy over what clothes I could or couldn't wear, I liked to pretend.

Thirty-seven minutes (hours?) and half the Old Testament later, Lyme admitted that he'd run out of questions. I aborted a grin. Had my trial ended? What did I win?

"In cases like this," he said, "what we usually find is that the patient has, or had at one point, allowed someone close to them—a relative, perhaps—to engage them in inappropriate relations. You say you're close to your father, correct?"

My chest couldn't have constricted more if it tried, but I was distracted by the sick swirling feeling in the pit of my stomach. My eyes locked on Lyme's empty gaze. His long fingers formed a granite lattice, as cold and forbidding as the moon.

"That's a filthy thing to say."

"Are you saying I'm wrong?"

"Yes. I'm also saying that if you're the sort of normal person I'm expected to convert into, I have a better chance of getting into heaven as a pervert."

Lyme, apparently immune to abuse, suggested we spend the remainder of our time in prayer. I almost pointed out that Mummy had prayed at me for years with no success. That was how I ended up in Lyme's office in the first place. But if he wanted to shut his mouth and talk to God instead of me, who was I to stop him?

I enjoyed praying very much, though the Lord did not see fit to answer mine with a plague of slugs to invade Lyme's car or smite his watch. I could only hope He would compare my prayers and Lyme's side by side and decide that mine outdid his in sincerity. I focused on the clock, hands still clasped, a very different prayer entering my mind. The moment all three hands pointed up, I walked out.

Dad waited in the car, a book propped against the steering wheel. His eyes seemed distant, scanning the horizon with nothing resembling interest. They snapped to me as I clambered inside.

"Don't bother bringing me back," I said.

"Wasn't planning on it," he replied.

The engine rumbled to life as we pulled away. I watched the mirror to make sure Lyme's building was growing smaller. A man in bland clothing appeared from behind the building, carefully approaching the front door. I knew he must have been a kindly gardener or an innocent secretary returning from a smoke, and that Lyme couldn't possibly have followed us so fast. I still clasped the armrests until we turned a corner and everything vanished behind a jewellery shop. Ha.

The turn sent sunlight into my eyes, but our car bumped along in fits and starts. The road ahead must have been crowded and rough. I scrunched my eyes into slits and looked out the window. The sky burned blue, searing into the flock of glassy-eyed people on the sidewalk. My chest ached at the sight of them, jostling through life without even thinking to look up, so instead I watched a flock of collared doves take flight.

Small Hours on the High Plains
David Goodrich

The Great Plains don't just appear. They sneak up on you in the middle of the night.

It had been a long day on the Katy Trail, an old railroad bed set up as a bicycle trail, with 74 miles of intermittent drizzle along the Missouri River. I was riding a loaded bike, panniers front and rear, from Delaware to Oregon. By western Missouri, the trees were beginning to scatter out a bit. I was looking forward to a bed for the night, but the only motel in town was booked. So I turned toward the campground along the river. Trisha, the host, could tell I'd had a long day as I walked out with an armful of food from the camp store.

"We've got some beautiful sites down on the river, but it's rising pretty steady. Supposed to crest tomorrow. Best camp on the back side of the levee."

The ride across had always spoken to me. It seemed straightforward on the map. Dip tire in right-hand ocean. Ride to left-hand ocean. To awaken each morning with a little smile, look up at nylon tent walls, and try to remember where I am. In Travels with Charley, Steinbeck wrote of smelling salt air after he crested the Cascade passes. I wondered if that was so.

By the time I reached the Katy Trail campground I was 1400 miles in, and the Missouri was at record levels. The surging river was the background for the night, a low powerful rumble. It was a message from a thousand miles upstream, from the mountains where I was bound, where record snowfall over the winter was melting rapidly. I lay down in the tent, almost too exhausted to sleep, and listened to a sonata in three movements. The first:

about ten, supercharged pickups, roaring down the river road, g-strings for mufflers. They quieted down after a while, and just as I was drifting off, the second: a distant train from across the river, whistle at a crossing, fading off into the distance. The third would wake me up from a very deep sleep: yips and squeals and barks, very close. It would take a howl from one for me to recognize that they were coyotes. Welcome to the West.

Before the trip, I had debated about whether to bring along a can of pepper spray. A few days on, a Missouri back road provided an occasion when I needed it. Missouri marks their roads with letters, and I stopped to take a picture of the sign for "Route ZZ." Then I noticed that a pack of a half-dozen dogs were accumulating about a ways up the road. They were barking continuously and looked as though they wanted a piece of me, or several. First I decided to wait and let them calm down. The owner would surely come out and get them, yes? No. Plan B involved waiting for a car to come and have it pass me just as I'm going past the dogs: sort of an Odysseus and the Cyclops move. Elegant, but one problem: no cars. Now was the time for the pepper spray. I rode up the road to gather some speed, then headed past them. Sure enough, they were all after me. The lead dog was right off to the left of my rear wheel. A stream of pepper spray took him out and a couple of his friends. A nice shot, I must say. But an overachiever was moving up fast on the right. I concentrated on pouring it on as I headed up the hill, my legs beginning to scream. Adrenaline works even after a day of riding. Gradually, the dog dropped off, and a burst of energy carried me the rest of the way to the night's campground. I thought of Churchill's quote: "There is nothing so exhilarating than to be shot at without result."

The morning after was clear and bright, calm for a change, and I was flying along after crossing into Kansas. I got a little too frisky. There was a bit of traffic at the railroad crossing. The rules for riding a bike across train tracks are simple: go perpendicular to the rails. But, worried about the traffic behind me, I took a short cut and began to cross the tracks at the same shallow angle as the cars. The front wheel dropped into the gap next to the rail with a thud. I was instantly pitched over the bars and onto the jagged rocks of the rail bed. Dazed, I took stock of the damage. Cycling gloves saved my hands, but blood was beginning to fill cuts on my shins. Things began to happen fast. I looked up and saw a light down the tracks. Hate it when that happens. The bell sounded and the crossing gates lowered. The whistle on the locomotive blew. Time to move quickly. I dragged the bike, mercifully intact, under the gate in time for the train to pass.

Down the street was a convenience store with a table inside. I pulled out my first aid kit to clean up, getting a suspicious look from the clerk. Unsaid: Don't worry, I won't bleed on the linoleum.

In planning the ride across Kansas back East at my desk, I had consciously increased the intended mileage per day from 60 to 80. It's flat, right? I would have reconsidered if I had known the etymology of the word. Kansas comes from the Sioux meaning "people of the south wind." For the entire ride across Kansas I would be battling the wind, going from cross winds to 30 mph in my face. I took a rest day in the town of Ottawa when winds over 40 were forecast. The low point came when I met the hundreds of riders of the Bike Across Kansas tour – headed east with the wind at their backs. Many waves and comments of "Aren't you going the wrong way?"

Exhausted and dehydrated, I had pulled into the tiny town of Tribune in the early afternoon, stopping at the only motel for dozens miles. The office smelled a bit like the retriever who appeared a few minutes later, and the owner had a multi-day beard. He was quite kind and assured me that the room had wifi and a hot shower. I rolled the bike around to the back of the motel and kicked the tumbleweed away from the door. There was barely space to get the bike in, with one light for the tiny room. And no signal. I mentioned the wifi situation at the office as I went out in search of liquid. The owner rubbed his chin.

Later that afternoon I had passed out on the bed. A high-pitched grinding sound right above my head made me jump up. It was coming from the next room. From the wall. Coming through the wall.

Half-groggy, I made a quick inventory of my defenses. I turned to face the wall, pepper spray and Swiss Army knife in hand, shoulders clenched. The grinding was getting louder. A small chunk of plaster flew out of the wall onto the dresser. The head of a drill emerged from the hole and retreated. Then a wire crawled out of the hole and began to snake down the wall. An Ethernet cable.

A muffled, matter-of-fact voice came through the wall. "That do you okay?"

"Uh. Uh. Sure. I'm sure that'll be just fine. Uh, thanks very much." And I stopped shaking.

There's not much going on in Tribune at 4:30AM. That was when I walked my bike across Route 96 into the cone of white florescent light that was Eagle Travel and Convenience, the only place with a semblance of breakfast across the wide expanse of plains. The heat had forced me into an early start on this leg of the cross-country ride. The day before had been the worst yet. Passing the Bike Across Kansas people, the thermometer had hit 1050 with a hard steady wind in my face. The only choice was to ball up as low as I could on the bike and drive into it, going piti-fully slow and stopping every few miles to drink. Water had been drawn out of my body at frightening speed, and I was going through five bottles a day.

This is wheat country, and epicenter of the Dust Bowl back in the 1930's. Then, years of drought had lead to dust storms "black as the inside of a dog," as one farmer put it, and people stuffed wet rags into cracks in the walls to keep the grit out. The summer of 2011 was nowhere as severe, but the maps showing drought had an ominous red patch stretching down from Kansas into Texas and west into Arizona. The morning sky was brown the day before: smoke from the huge Wallow fire in Arizona, 600 miles to the west.

Over hundreds of years, drought isn't uncommon in the West. Records from tree rings tell us there have been more severe droughts that preceded the Dust Bowl, well before the era of rapid rise of greenhouse gases. But the unmistakable rise in temperature tilts the odds in favor of drought, especially in the southern Plains. It's not so complicated. Warmer air holds more water and evaporates more, drying out the land. It also makes for longer and more severe fire seasons in the West. I had already seen the smoke drifting across the sky.

After battling the shimmering heat the day before, I had resolved to get an early start, to make use of every precious minute of the cool, calm morning hours. Crossing the highway, shadows of grain elevators leaned into the starlight. My eyes squinted in the jagged light of the convenience store. Microwave breakfast burritos were the only selection. One would be plenty. I took my coffee and paper plate to the cashier and paid.

"Any chance of the weather breaking sometime soon?" I asked.

He smiled and shook his head. "You know what they say. Put a twenty under a glass of water on a fence post first thing. By ten, the water'll be gone."

I found a plastic table, behind a couple of men in dungarees wearing baseball caps with the names of farms on the front. Later in the morning these farmers would be in the cabs of combines, moving over the fields like giant bugs. I listened in on the conversation.

"What's the yield looking like for you boys?" one asked.

"Best guess right now is down about 30%, and it'll be all we can do to get there."

"I wish I was just down 30%. That might just get it done." He paused to look out the window. "They say you gotta get big to survive, but my wife says our bills are $20,000 this month with fuel and fertilizer and John Deere."

Kansas is a place of tough, hospitable people making a living off a hard land. In a changing climate, it won't get easier. The 2011 summer broke all kinds of records. In both 2011 and 2012, ranchers liquidated large herds because there wasn't enough food or water. From the air, much of Kansas is filled with green circles, the mark of center pivot irrigation. The farmers at Eagle Travel and Convenience pump water from the ground to water their crops, but it's not clear how long the water will last. In parts of southwest Kansas, the aquifer has been drawn down by over 150 feet since irrigation began.

My stomach was grumbling from the burrito as I went out into the parking lot. I got on the bike and turned west once again, first light to my back, into the hot, dry, blast furnace wind already spinning up for the day.

Against Penetration
Paul Grams

Mike drove us to the ocean   yesterday
dirt track for miles   then widened all the world
sand water sand and water sky sky sky
taint nothing here   and dang so much of it
I sat with chica   ocean lapped its way
cold dull inexorable   to where our thighs
held our hot living hmms   night whispered child
unclench youselves   the universe wont hurt

I killed my cousin once   gunshock to the head
I been eleven   found Bug's shit   Mike says
I wake him up   you scare him   pop   night whispered
you let him out   watch him come out   was screaming
cant say so much   fuck was like I just dreaming
and auntie put the blood on me   said this word
out   kept apart unemptied how it is
not dippin into darkness   opened dead

Must We Wait on Later to See the Right?
Paul Grams

Lord   if it be some kind of heaven where
us gon go who   be meek and took most kind
of screaming at and shit   who took ten
steps back when some damn in-the-wrong been
nine steps in my face   lord if some stand this night
of worldclass misuse   and dont go stupid blind
and murder some dog   cause they aint gon share

Lord let us swagger some while we got legs
enjoy this only dance   man been knock down
damn concrete gon misuse you palms   I swear
too often them with gates and guns   aint fair
I knock who wouldnt open   put it down
earth here for who dont threat or either beg

Old Man With a Cane
Jeff Hardin

So old his steps are inches at a time
so that it takes him minutes to advance

across the parking lot to find his car.
A cane he touches out ahead to see

if he should stop, change course, continue on.
Whatever pleading holds his feeble frame

upright, whatever tenderness allows
him space upon this earth, I now applaud.

And that he ever came to be at all,
diminished as he is, is cause enough

to get up casually and wander toward
the place he's getting closer to, then turn,

say, "Lovely day" and "Let me get that door
for you" and "Isn't this the sweetest life?"

To Begin

Jeff Hardin

Toward
    some shape of sense emerging,
        some newness,
    this small-self begins,
      self of what next, self of
          lean into this aching ache to know—
how, when, why—not knowing exactly how or when or why.

Some
    claim everything in the universe
        is the only size possible,

      held forth and held together
        by laws I sometimes think
          I understand and then
  as quickly lose. And the fact a person ever exists at all is
overwhelming
    in implications,
        statistically almost impossible,
      yet here I am,
        troubling the still waters
          of what troubles me,
  attempting, yet again, to balance joy against the constant
question
    of when I'll cease to be.
        Small-question, I know,
        and really beside the point,
          since simply being here
            astounds me, though I
make no disturbance, though my questions turn to awe.

As Much or As Little
Jeff Hardin

With
    another spring upon me,
        redbuds out back

        beginning to catch fire,
            I feel more *here*
                than ever,

sealed to this life, this little time I have been given.

All
    I ask is what
        I ask and ask again—

        for more, for less,
            for as much or as little
                as I can bear.

I still believe, as I've said before, that all

creation
    knows we walk among it;
        it sends, as needed,

        the sun or shade, wind
            or stillness. Even so,
                what role is mine?

    blessed observer before it all? participant? Shouldn't

    I,
        too, bend all I am,
                reach toward the light,

            let loose my limbs
                in flung-out ecstasy
                    like forsythia down by the road?

    I know I'd look silly, but so what. Why is it we'll

sing
    in total abandon
             about a love once lost,

        a broken heart, while all around us,
            answering our ache,
                a plenty abounds?

We note it, if at all, and go on, missing the call to join in.

What The River Says
Jeff Hardin

That
    I have risen
        yet another morning

      to have this sense
        of being in the world
          and gone on up the hill

  to look so wide and far in all directions

is
    one more mystery
        of time's unfolding

      I guess I cannot know.
      That I remain
        while others fell away

  is God's great secret, the pleasure of His will.

"What
    is man that you are
        mindful of him,"

      David asked,
        and so did Job,
          our lives compared to vapor,

  to grass, to fig, to lamb, to bread.

    I
        have only the same question,
                asked in what I hope

            is a tone of wonder,
              a tone of submission,
                though I know, too, knowing myself,

    I hold a part back, my own secret. What I

say
        is what I cannot
                find my way to say,

    though it be before me,
        this next moment, its stillness,
            where my foot may find

    firm footing, or may, in due time, slip, and then be led away.

Estuary
Peleg Held

There the waters gather between childhood and sea,
vetted through the gratings, half-fettered and half-free,

rivulets of duct and dream, of pore and bedded vein
speaking in a pupal hum, the moaning of low names

before we come to waves, before we drop our wings
like yellow leaves into a current that carries all it thins.

They pass beneath the arch, the rudiment of eyes,
adrift upon the rivered night, all under on the rise.

Tuned to curves of tunnel-black, curled, the fallen, shine
and dancing, spin to beg the river hurry to the brine

where the waters gather between the faithful and the sea
guttered through the gratings, clawed of certainty.

Waters born of cleft and stitch, of wound and ruddied rain,
ink to mark the chrysalis walls in glory and in pain.

Lines for Possum
Ryan Hibbett

So you didn't come back as a yellow butterfly.
You looked beautiful anyway, hunched
on the privacy fence, your eyes
like nuggets of hematite giving back
the porch light, and your whitish fur spiked
delicately by the winter air. Nothing at all
like the possum dad beat from the garage
with a corn broom, showing his blood-lined
gums as he back-pedaled into the lilacs.

I've seen the plump cords of tail
waggling into the night, and caught
glints of light from faraway eyes,
but you simply stayed put near the window,
watching your family sip wine and rummage
through photographs just days after your
departure. Your old life must have looked
strange, as you studied the tears
in your twin's eyes, and saw hunks
of birthday cake parceled out; I hope
you weren't cold, or too confused when
your son-in-law choked on the pot roast.

Eventually we had to recognize you,
and even as we closed in, wolf-like,
you kept still, your lake-black eyes
holding the night. You looked so sad. I'm
sorry my cousin blew into your face,
and know that it took all you had not to hiss,

watching your lips part slightly
into the grimace you used to give
sluggish baggers in the check-out line.

Now it's clear your possum transformation
was underway when you hobbled
from the hospital for the last time, your voice
shrunk to a rasp, your face chiseled
with weeks of not eating. You were
beyond their care, your hopes reduced
at last to a local shaman who burnt sage
around your bed. Finally you requested
morphine and played dead, rolling
your eyes back and letting your mouth
drop to expose the small, angular teeth
you had flossed nightly right to the end.

I called you Possum when you turned
your head in disbelief that I would
wreck your slumber, a brash child
who didn't care how early you had to rise,
who had a question maybe, and wasn't
fooled for one second by the squinting
eyes or the bared incisors
as you stirred to listen.

The Exact Heart of Mesopotamia
Amy Holman

You can't leave life without much
trouble, the inexact heart remarks.
Cultural differences touch

the border -- and explode -- such
divisions. Archaeologist envisions parks.
You can't leave life without much

secret, whispers the elaborate hutch
of Mesopotamia below 1,000 blasted works.
Cultural differences touch

upon a point: is man on a crutch
or buried? To excavate ruin harks
you can't leave life without much

horror. Bodies blown dislodge
spires, pathways. A city, layered, unlocks
culture. Real differences. Touch

the worlds we lost. Heritage
resurrects us, briefly joined in the flux.
You can't leave life without much
cultural differences -- or touch.

    Note: The title is the phrase used by Nejat Kocer, deputy of the Dept of Justice and Development in Gazientep, Turkey, to describe an Iron Age ruin about to be excavated after the last of 1,200 land mines were removed from the border with Syria. (Source: *Archaeology News Network* quoting *Today's Zaman* September 30, 2011)

A Common Land

Jane Hoogestraat

So much remains unknown, the story of gold
buried in a corner never found, though an aunt heard
he died with something on his conscience. Every family
has its dark lore, a shade lifting in a deserted farm house,
a rafter in an abandoned barn wiped clean, he was
talking to himself in the fields some times.

Though their arrowheads don't surface anymore,
Yankton Sioux once lived along the nearby river--
a genealogy of two cultures, traces of tribal language
and Platt Deutsch both fading, almost gone.
The harvest moon hangs taunting
a parched cloud, no romance in these fields just now.

My uncle died young working here, 1987 when
climate change baked doubt away, futures skyrocketed,
contracts were bought back. There have been good years
since then, heavy snowfalls, spring rain. But not this one,
corn stalks not worth the harvest, fissures in sloughs,
no gold, nights that breathe dry the horizon's last light.

A Drawn and Papered Heart

Beth Konkoski

2013 F. Scott Fitzgerald Short Story Contest Winner

It pays fifty bucks an hour, and the class is three and a half hours long. Not the sort of thing you tell your mother about, but we'll make rent. And it isn't as bad as I expected. I was nervous, but the first night, we stopped for dinner and after two beers and some enchiladas, I relaxed. I told Richard about the zit on my back. "Will they notice? Draw it?"

"It isn't about perfection," he said finishing his third Corona. Do colleges care about professors drinking before class?

Tonight I slip out of my jeans and into the white robe I have carried over the mountain to this community college in the desert. Richard teaches Life Drawing 201 here at night after a day of high school art classes because they hire him and college teaching looks good on his resume. But he complains. "Nobody down here willing to model. How do you teach a fucking life drawing class without a model?"

And that is where I fit in. The curtained space I stand in has art room props on a shelf behind me: dried flowers, a paper mache dog sculpture, a tarnished silver ice bucket, arms and legs from a mannequin. It is a small, thrown together changing room, the size of a shower, comforting the first night when I was so nervous about undressing, but now I feel a little foolish, hiding back here to transform from person to model. Why don't I just take off my clothes and leave them in a pile by the stool? I guess that would feel more intimate, letting my jeans slide off my thighs in front of the students, mostly young Mexican boys with perfect skin and hair that falls like rain when they take off their baseball caps. They are beautiful, each of them, but especially Antonio. I try to find poses that will keep me looking his direction, able to see the squinting, dense focus that crosses his face when he draws me.

Before stepping on the wooden platform I look around on the shelves for props to hold. Last week Richard went nuts when I wrapped my arms through an empty wooden picture frame, its gilded surface shedding gold paint on my shoulder. "The angles, the angles," he proclaimed, making me shift at least five times with my body contorted inside the rectangle. I had expected modeling to be dull, maybe some time to think a little about the three classes I still need to take for my Master's in Special Ed. so I don't lose my job. Then there's the visit from my parents to worry about; their attitude toward Luke has not improved since the wedding and they will require an especially well-planned story if I am to cover up his ill-fated military career and current job as a surfer of channels in our apartment. It isn't like I'm ok with where he's at; I'm just trying to have a little patience.

Anyway, the hours on this small stage aren't slow or empty at all. I realized the first night, hot under the lights and keeping my calves flexed while I crouched on the edge of the stool, that I am part of the finished product in an active sense. Somehow my energy shows up on their pages, and the drawings are always better when I focus on how I am positioned and who is drawing me. I have to push the pose out at them and think about it, watching the sweep of the second hand on the clock so I move on a schedule: eight poses at thirty seconds, six at two minutes, four at four minutes and two at six minutes. We run through this pattern then take a break. The second session begins with four minutes and moves to the final, almost impossible sixteen that feels like six hundred. When my mind drifts, Richard knows. When I walk around the easels on break and see what they draw, I can tell the poses that deflated or kept me too much in my head.

There is a vase tucked behind a pile of duck decoys, and I pull it toward me. The bottom scrapes like finger nails on the metal shelf and kicks up art dust, a mix of all their erasing and scribbling and sharpening. It smells of brush cleaner, chalk and failure this dust that settles on my arms and travels deep into my lungs when I pose. The vase is large enough to hug and painted with metallic gold paint. I don't believe it has held flowers in this decade as it smells dry as a late summer creek.

A single rose sits across the stool. The outer petals curl like a lipsticked mouth, just a small pout off the head of the bloom. I touch its velvet, then lift it from the stool and look around. Antonio's eyes meet mine above his easel.

"For Valentine's," he says. And his gaze returns to the page even though he has nothing yet to sketch. A pulse kicks alive in my groin and at my collarbone, like I've been doing a quick set of jumping jacks. At the stool I cannot quite decide what to do with the rose or the vase, and the lights are small lasers on the back of my head, their heat traveling through my hair to spike me.

"We're ready?" Richard asks. The students step to their easels and face me. The rose and vase are an impossible match. The mouth would hold three dozen, so I place the single one on the floor and let my robe slip off as well. I balance on the stool with my legs out like a frog's, the vase hugged tightly against my breasts, my face turned so a cheek touches the rim. I stare at nothing on the classroom wall.

Antonio's rose has reminded me that I did not buy Luke a card for Valentine's Day, our second as a married couple. But he has been so difficult since his discharge, not even waking up when I leave for work, on the couch with Styrofoam takeout boxes beside him when I get home. He seems like a different person these last months and helping him feels both awkward and exhausting, especially since he barely answers my questions about the simplest things like getting the mail or buying a paper for want ads. "I hear you" is his preferred response, if he answers at all. So the idea of romance has not been much on my mind, but still, six years together, two married and I blow it off. It is all I can think of for the thirty second poses, and this makes me hold them too long. Richard must cue me, cue me, cue me. The irritation is thick in his voice.

On the dining table when I was a child I would lay out all the Valentine cards in the box my mother had purchased, trying to match the message of the card with the right person from class. One year I couldn't decide on the card for Robbie Gleason who had come up behind me on the playground and grabbed my elbows, pulled me to him and whispered, "Will you go out with me?" The only place to go in the fifth grade was the skating rink, so we spent the winter skating circles together after his hockey practice, my hand clenched in his through mittens so thick we could have been holding wooden sticks. As the rink shut down one Friday night, we skated a circle in the dark and he snowplowed in the far corner, pulling me into the shadows where he pressed me against the wood, his cold lips like a flint the instant they touched mine. I can see myself at the table searching for the right card, getting annoyed as I shuffled and reshuffled, finally randomly putting them in envelopes and signing names on the front only. Nothing on those cards could tell him how his kiss had made me think of summer and warm coals even as the wind blew against us. And I was scared to give him something noticeable, something from the drugstore in town that would state things clearly. On Valentine's Day he left a heart-shaped box of chocolates on my desk—To Shelly, From Robbie. The box was still in the closet of my old room; he had not been afraid.

"Michelle." The voice pulls at me, and I jerk myself off the stool. "Please." Richard's impatience and superiority are a vapor in the room. He points to the clock with his sharp, goateed chin, an artsy look he cannot pull off, and scolds me with the narrowing of his eyes. I am glad I turned down his suggestion that we sleep together after class the first night. At the time I felt a little bad about how harsh I sounded saying no, but he knows I'm married. More importantly, he is at least fifteen years older than me, and I don't think I hid that thought very well. His face sort of emptied and he mumbled, "Of course not," as he led us to his car. In the teacher's lounge at school the next day, he apologized without looking at me, but wanted to know if I would still model. "You're good, and I don't want to lose a model or be weird with a colleague," he said before walking away. I wondered how sleeping together would have left us "not weird," but it wasn't really worth going into. Luke wouldn't have liked me still riding over the mountain with him if he knew about the proposition, but I am not in the habit of telling him everything I experience. I have assessed the risk and weighed the options; I'm pretty sure I can overpower Richard if he ever presses it, so I don't worry. I turn my focus to the clock and the angles of my body until break.

"I liked your shoulders in this one." Jose points, and I see the solid twist of torso, a neck long and looking away. They never draw more than an outline, a suggestion of me in space. Richard says they are learning how the body connects and doesn't, how different it looks from what they expect. I hear him telling a student that he wasn't looking carefully, hadn't really seen. Tightening the belt on my robe, I step away from the circle and into the hall. I will walk to the bathroom for something to do.

"You didn't look at mine tonight." His voice sounds like wings in the dark.

"Sorry." I step to where he leans against a bank of windows. Outside the sun has turned everything to some scrambled art tapestry of orange and vomit pink. The clouds look like crumpled laundry.

We are only a few feet apart, and I can see a pulse in his throat. His arms cross at his heart and he doesn't look away. He has been in my thoughts all night; if I'm honest, before tonight. I want to dig around in the space behind his eyes, to feel the shine of his hair across my skin.

"Thank you for the rose."

"You're welcome. He looks me in the eyes now. " Valentine's Day is for beauty." The classroom door opens, and we are both startled by Richard searching, spotting, scowling.

"Time," he says like a referee. Antonio hustles himself toward the call, so I am unable to say anything. I just follow, watch him move in his jeans and let his words repeat inside my head. For the second half of class I am anchored on the stage, imagining what Antonio will think of each pose, how he will shift me onto paper. Even the sixteen minute ones feel short as I breathe my way around what I will say to him after class. At the end of the night there is never an inspection of work, just the hurry to be done and away. But if I dress quickly, I should be able to catch him in the parking lot while Richard closes up the room.

The night is almost chilly when I step outside. I can see a group of them walking together toward the scattered cars in the lot. Their voices sound as young as kids on a playground as they toss goodbyes around. I hurry to catch up. Antonio peels off toward a pick-up truck near one of the light posts. I am ready to call his name when the passenger door opens. High heels click on pavement.

"Antonio?" And then a spectacular girl in a leather mini dress emerges from behind the truck's cab. Her body flashes through the dark like a meteor in its confidence and layered gold. "It took so long," she says.

"Gloria." He steps toward her, kisses her with his arms cupping her chin. She wraps herself around him, into him, a little leap and her legs circle his waist. He boosts her higher on his hips and kisses her harder. They crash against the side of the truck, and I can hear them both moan. I am grateful for the dark and the moment of not calling his name. Back on the sidewalk, I drop Antonio's rose in the blue recycle container and pace quietly in the shadows, waiting for Richard who will drive us back over the mountain.

The Bodies in the Bridges
Rachel Kubie

A republic of loosely stacked cobblestone spines
scattering its path into the woods. A people's
consent plentiful as dogwood, drifting a white calm
in the green sleep of afternoon shadows. We won't
fix it, we won't fix it. The rain in the evening
doesn't startle us, because we were expecting it.
I would organize the thistle in its sharp bouquets
to show the natural dignity in the thick green spears
at the edges of the fields. I would organize my own
wonder for something more useful. What we call each bloom
is what the blossom comes to in our imaginations,
our nations of wildflower, nations of ragweed,
nations of scattering seed. All rustling softly into evening.

Arithmetic
Gerry LaFemina

On the phone chatting about New Orleans

with a woman–she mentions beignets,
Bourbon Street, beads, says she'll ride me

bareback on a king-sized bed. I'm thinking

fourth grade math: less than, unequal to.
I'm thinking Cuba & you in a floral two piece,

blue Caribbean & the secret police. Taste

of mango & lime on your tongue, you
who's never wondered about my hands, never

a second glance. You're with a new guy, his lips

on your ankle, your calf. This is the thing
I don't get about longing, its merciless

imagination. I'm trying to want coffee

laced with chicory, trying to want her
skin beneath my fingertips. Oh the complicated

possibilities of desire. Oh, the story problems–

love is not five mangoes, so don't ask me how
many I've given away, how many I have left.

A Mammoth Lamentation
Martin H. Levinson

You trip on my trunk, brush by my tail,
crash over my legs, are nicked by my tusks,
yet you act as if I am not there.

What have I done to deserve
such scorn and contempt? Why am
I the pariah at the party?

I've got feelings and they get hurt when
you do not acknowledge my existence, to wit
Johnny's a drug addict,

Mary's cheating on her husband,
Ralph didn't die from natural causes,
he killed himself.

Is it so hard to admit that population growth
threatens the planet, that war is good for business, that
democracy is not a perfect system, that climate change is real.

I don't want encomiums or
compliments, just some candor and
a little sincerity that will keep me

from becoming the emperor's new clothes,
an 800-pound gorilla, a woebegone
elephant trapped in a room.

Names
Peter Makuck

My father, recovering from surgery
before TVs were the hospital room norm,
said, *Listen, I'm paying for your education.*
      Get me something good to read.

In college then, I first tried Hemingway
on this Polish auto mechanic
but on my next visit, he said,
      This is baby talk,
and did an imitation that made me laugh.

So I told him Einstein thought
      The Brothers Karamazov
was the best novel ever written.
      Fine, he said, *I'll give it a try*
And loved it—the only novel he ever read.

At our garage, under a car
with a grease gun, I overheard him
once ask a customer/teacher,
      Have you ever read . . .
Then describe Fyodor, the horny old buffoon,
Dmitri in a troika madly hunting Grushenka . . .

Again spending time with the Karamazovs
I realize this morning
that with names and nicknames
      Russian and Polish come close.
Names so hard for my students

posed no problem for my father,
for in *Babcia's* farmhouse kitchen,
pet names for my cousins, uncles,
and aunts swooped about
like exotic birds: Vanka, Vlad, Lidka.
And for me too: Piotr,
       Piotrek, Petrush,
Petruska, and more.

Hardy's Soldier
William Miller

In a neighbor's garden.
they dug up the remains
of a Roman soldier.
Hardy was a boy and pushed
his way through
the crowd to see.
A small round shield
was on his chest,
darkened like the helmet
by centuries in
the gray ground.
A short sword lay
by his side.
Hardy never forgot those
bones, that sword, not as an
architect, not as a young
or old writer.
Those bones were his muse:
the past never the past
but there, in the garden,
just below the surface.
He turned the soil
to find what wasn't supposed
to be there, long buried,
forgotten.
Stories, poems were
written about the ancient
mounds and tall carved stones,
the lives of common folk
as mysterious....

The soldier's bones were
buried quickly; the crowd
went home.

But Hardy lingered
by the mound,
still saw Rome
in Wessex clay.

The Bottle Tree
William Miller

In this photograph,
a boy sits on
a sagging step
of his front porch.
He looks away
from the bottle tree,
as if he had no
faith in it to stop
evil spirits from
reaching the house.
Maybe he looks
down a dirt road
to the nearest
town, a bus that
runs north and south.
He doesn't want
to grow old in a

young man's body,
live in fear of
the next cool,
summer....
We might claim
blood-ties as he
is old enough to be
our father or
grandfather.

                        And many of us are
                        restless today,

chased by something
we can't name.

Evil spirits, trapped
in glass or not,
never die.

Everything You Ever Wanted

Dan Moreau

For an upgrade he'll throw in a mistress on the side. "If you're into that sorta thing," the salesman says. "How much?" I say. He sucks in his cheeks. "For you. A decent mistress. One who isn't needy or make demands, I'd say another ten thou." "Fine. I'll take it. How about the secure protection plan?" "You beat me to the sales pitch. No family is complete with our state of the art, twenty-four-seven secure protection plan. It'll ensure the safety of your loved ones so you never lose sleep over who might be lurking outside your window." "Cut the spiel. I'll take it." He rings me up, punching the numbers on an adding machine: wife, two children (one boy, one girl), decent job, two-story house on a cul-de-sac with a yard and a tree, two cars, a lap dog, a mistress on the side, secure protection. He shows me the total on the adding machine. I let out a wolf whistle. "Happiness doesn't come cheap, does it?" he says. I nod and call my bank to authorize the wire transfer of my entire life savings.

My new name is Burt Wiggins. You can customize everything but the name is non-negotiable. It's like buying a car. You can't change the name. The Burt Wiggins is one of the most popular plans. It's what everyone thinks will make them happy, a house in the suburbs, fourth of July barbecues, little league, wife and kids, Sunday dinner, a small lap dog, a small to moderately severe drinking problem. It's what our forefathers wanted and they didn't have to shell out a small fortune for it. It was practically handed to them on a platter after World War II. Here's your home, your job, wife and kids. Anything else? My generation didn't have it so lucky. Middle class is rarefied air. It's like peach cobbler, from what I hear. Soft and sweet and juicy with just the right amount of tang. I've never actually tasted peach cobbler.

After dropping me off in front of the house the salesman jangled the keys in front of me. "You're all set to go."

I glanced at him, grabbed the keys and opened the car door. From the sloping driveway I surveyed my new domain. Quiet. The best silence money could buy, no noise from a jackhammer, no truck backing up, no car alarm, no loud neighbors. I opened the mailbox and retrieved a bundle of catalogs, bills and credit card solicitations, the pleasures of owning a home: everyone wants to lend you more money you can't afford. The bundle tucked under my arm, I paused on the threshold ready to knock when I realized I had a key. Wiping my feet on the Welcome mat, I entered my new life.

"Honey, I'm home," I bellowed.

The interior was the kind I had seen in movies and read about in books, an interior I had glimpsed in dreams: beige wall-to-wall carpeting, a paisley couch in the living room, a big-screen television nestled inside an entertainment center, family pictures on the mantel piece and central air that made the house cool enough for a sweater in the summer and warm enough to go barefoot in the winter. Mingled with the lemony scent of Pledge was the smell of a slow-cooking roast in the kitchen.

"Honey, you're home," a woman said, appearing in an apron over a polka-dot dress that showed off her calves. Shoulder-length honey brown hair, cute face, nice rack, ample hips—just like the model in the showroom. The popular Debra model, her curves, hair color and lips all rigorously market tested to every man's desire and who made one helluva meatloaf. She was the ideal housewife, not too pretty but pretty enough with just the right sex drive, wanting a roll in the hay without being a nympho, who'd gladly administer BJs on special occasions, birthdays, anniversaries, and romantic evenings without the kids.

She kissed me and I squeezed her waist. "Burt," she said. "Save it for the bedroom. Kids! Your father's home. Dinner's almost ready, dear."

There followed a rumble down the carpeted stairs that sounded like stampede.

"Daddy!"

Wrapped in a hug by Amanda, eleven. Not old enough to be dating (Thank God) but young enough to enjoy running through sprinklers and playing dress up. Beloved of her teachers, straight-A student on the honor roll. In the showroom, I paged through her brochure, flipping through the trajectory of her life from first boyfriend to first heartache, from high school to college, from her first job to her wedding. All these things, toasting her wedding, giving her away as a bride, being her shoulder to cry on when things were rough with her husband, enjoying the soft warmth of her body against mine, all these things I could look forward to.

"Hey Dad," said Eric coolly, thirteen. Already a spectacular athlete. An all around good kid who looked out for his sister, mowed the lawn and hit the books pretty hard.

According to the brochure, there would be some bumps in the road, a little pot, a little alcohol, wrecking the car at fifteen but thankfully no injuries beyond minor scratches and bruises. We'd play catch in the yard. In due time, I'd give him the talk, sitting on the foot of his bed, hands clasped between my knees, head bowed like a penitent. The awkwardness would melt away once I suggest I take him out for ice cream.

Last but not least came Fritz bounding along, bringing up the rear, pawing at my knees until I picked him up, a miniature black Schnauzer. I couldn't believe all this was mine. I put down Fritz and sat at the head of the table. Debra smiled at me and I smiled back as I took hers and Amanda's hand and we bowed our heads and gave thanks for the bounty before us, for our good health and for the safety and wellbeing of our loved ones. Amen.

After dinner Debra hummed in the kitchen as she loaded the dishwasher. The kids sat enraptured in front of the TV, their faces aglow, watching age appropriate content, nothing that would scar their impressionable young minds or give them bad dreams. I stepped out into the backyard. The sun was setting, the grass and tree from which hung a swing awash in purple light. Two Adirondack chairs looked out over the garden, from which I could see Debra and myself growing old together, holding hands during sunset, a fleece blanket pulled into our laps. On a support beam that held up the porch awning I noticed a fleck of hardened white paint on it. I pulled at it and it unraveled like a long piece of tape.

That night, the kids finally tucked away, I closed the door to our bedroom. Debra stood in front of a full length mirror, taking off her earrings. I watched my hands encircle her waist as I kissed the back of her neck.

"Burt," she said.

"What?"

She tapped my hand. "Not tonight, O.K. honey?"

"Sure," I said, letting her go. "You owe me a rain check."

The next morning I sat down at the breakfast table. Amanda and Eric were eating cereal with milk. I yawned. "Where's breakfast?"

Eric slid a box of cereal across the table toward me.

"Doesn't Mom make you breakfast?" I said.

Amanda shook her head while slurping the bottom of her bowl. "She likes to sleep in. Sorry gotta go, Dad. I'll miss my bus."

"How about you, Eric? Need a ride?"

"I'm biking, Dad"

Alone in the kitchen, I ate Eric's leftover soggy cereal. In the glove compartment of my new Toyota Prius—new to me at least—were driving directions and a clip-on ID badge. I'd told the lifestyle salesman I wanted a job with minimal responsibility, one where I could surf the net all day and make personal calls. I parked in front of a non- descript office park with trimmed hedges, an artificial pond and the company name—Naltrech—slapped on a bed of marble outside. Bored looking yard workers chased leaves with blowers from one end of the parking lot to the other. Inside, at the security desk, flashing my badge I said I had forgotten my keys. The guard showed me to my office. It had a view of the parking lot, a computer, a phone, a picture of my family, a stress relief ball, and sticky notes with hearts drawn by my daughter decorating my monitor. I checked the drawers. Papers, file folders, napkins, paperclips, plastic utensils and packets of soy sauce and ketchup. Bored after a few hours of surfing porn and news sites, I ventured out of my office in search of the coffee room.

"Hey Brad," a clean-cut guy in a tie said in the hall.

"Hey," I said.

"How are the quarterlies coming?"

"They're coming," I said.

"Well, great to see ya. Catch you on the flip side."

"Asshole," I muttered under my breath.

The air handler rumbled on and pumped cool air into my office. Outside the window, the yard men continued blowing around leaves in the parking lot. I sipped my coffee. The wall clock ticked off the seconds like a reproach. The phone rang. "When can you come over?" a woman said.

"I'll be there in five."

In the glove compartment I found directions to her apartment. One of my keys unlocked her door. The apartment smelled like fresh paint and vanilla. She was lying on top of the bed spread in a satin negligee, scalloped at the hem and collar with pink lace. Just as the brochure had promised she was a curvaceous brunette with blue, mischievous eyes. "What took you so long?" she said.

"I got here as fast as I could."

She toyed with my hair. "Was it worth it? The upgrade," she said.

"Worth every cent."

My headlights illuminated the driveway, momentarily casting a cottontail's monstrous shadow on the garage door until it loped away. When I cut the engine, it was suddenly very dark and quiet. No lights were on in the house. I picked my way through the dark toward the front door careful not to trip on a crack in the driveway and split open my forehead.

"Hello?" I said. I loosened my tie and dropped my keys in a ceramic dish in the entryway. I picked up the dish wondering if it had a story, if Debra and I had bought it on a trip to Mexico or if it was a wedding gift or maybe just some chintzy thing she picked up on sale.

"Where is everybody?" I said.

It was late. A dark figure was slumped at the kitchen table. I was supposed to leave Lisa's house at five but she pulled me back to bed and we went at it for another hour. By the time I had showered and dressed, it was nearly eight. "Do you have to go?" she'd said. "Why don't you stay for dinner? We can order in." It sounded lovely but I had to go.

I switched on the hallway light. The figure stood up from the table and as he stepped toward me the light picked out his features. Frowning with downcast eyes, the salesman held up his hand before I could say anything.

"Don't tell me. I know. She wanted you to stay. It happens to all my clients the first time. What you have to understand is that you have to keep up appearances with the family. You can't just disappear for hours at a time. It can't be all about you. If Debra kicks you out, I can't do anything about it. This only works if you play your part too. This is the real deal. It isn't a fantasy. These are real people. Not to worry. I covered for you. I told Debra and the kids that you were working late and sent them out for pizza. They'll be home soon and I suggest you put your game face on."

He patted me on the shoulder and headed for the door.

"Thanks," I said. "It won't happen again."

He looked back and said, "Don't screw up." Moments later, Debra's car pulled into the drive. Eric and Amanda rushed through the door, Amanda shouting, "Daddy, Daddy, I missed you." I picked her up and spun her. Next came Debra holding a giant pizza.

"There you are." She kissed my cheek. "Working late again?"

"Quarterlies are due soon."

She stroked my chest. "Maybe tonight we can mess around."

I grinned. "It's a deal."

Later that night, I rolled off her and lay beside her in our darkened bedroom. The house sighed. Leaves rustled against the window. "Thanks, dear. That was wonderful."

She stared vacantly at the ceiling. The jagged shadow of the tree beyond our window danced on the ceiling.

"Is something wrong?" I said.

"It's like you were making love to me for the first time," she said. "Like I was completely new to you."

I leaned over and kissed her. "You're beautiful."

"You're not cheating on me, are you?"

"No, dear. What would make you say that?"

"Nothing. I don't look like what I used to."

"Stop it. You look amazing."

She turned on her side away from me. "Goodnight, dear."

"Goodnight."

In the morning I drove Eric to school. Slumped in his seat, he half dozed against the window, his shaggy brown hair curtained over his forehead. His lips were drawn thin and wide across his mouth. He had big brown eyes and long eyelashes the way boys do.

"So how are things?" I said.

"Fine," he said.

"What about your mom? How is she doing?"

"Are you moving out again?"

"No, why would I do that?"

"I dunno. Last week Mom said you weren't welcome in the house anymore."

I patted his leg. "Don't worry, chief. I'm not going anywhere."

After dropping off Eric at school I drove to work. Brittle leaves were scattered around the parking lot. Tie guy intercepted me in the hallway. "Hey Brad, those quarterlies ready?"

"Not yet," I growled.

"No rush. Whenever you're done. Rome wasn't built in a day, was it?"

"No, but it burned down in one."

"Touché!"

On my computer came an incoming video chat. I accepted. "What's wrong with you?" the salesman said. "That's guy's your boss. Can't you kiss his ass a little? I know this is a cushy gig but you have to do something. It's simple. Go through the quarterlies and match the entries with the ones online. It's that simple. If there's a discrepancy, eh. You can investigate it or not. Up to you. The bottom line is that you're killing me, Brad. You think it was easy to get this job? My reputation is on the line too. So man up and do your job."

I stuffed the quarterlies in a drawer and drove to my mistress's. There was no answer. I looked in the windows and banged on the door. Finally she answered, a flimsy silk kimono tied around her waist. "What's wrong with you?" she said.

Moreau | 85

I pushed past her into the apartment. A man in the bedroom was struggling into his pants.

"You can't be here," she said.

"How did you know I got an upgrade?"

She shrugged. "I don't know. I know about all my clients."

The man carried his shoes out of the apartment.

"So I'm a client?"

She crossed her arms and sighed. "Yes you are."

"Does my family know? Does my boss know?"

"Know what?"

"That this is fantasy?"

"It's not a fantasy. It's real, hun."

"Are you paid?"

"Of course, I'm paid. Do you think I do this for shits and giggles?"

From there I drove to the Life Center. Inside the glass walls, amid the brochures of identities (athletes, politicians, movie stars) and cardboard cutouts with holes in the face where you could pose and imagine yourself under your new identity, the salesman was huddled at a table with a couple, his head bent low in conference.

"I need to talk to you," I said.

"Can't you see I'm busy with a client?" He turned back to the couple. "Now, as I was saying we can make you a very famous couple. Brad and Angelina. Or more low key like a Ted Danson and Mary Steenburgen."

"Don't do business with this man. He's a fraud," I said.

The couple got up and started walking toward the door.

"Hold on," the salesman said chasing them. "Let's talk about this." He ran his fingers through his hair. "Thanks a lot. Are you going to pay me for that lost commission?"

"I want my old shitty life back."

"Sorry buddy, no can do. When you bought your new identity, you gave up your old one. It says right here in the paperwork you signed."

"What happened to it?"

"What do you think? Your life seems pretty shitty to you but someone else it's a dream. A roof over your head, a job, a car, food. Those are luxuries to some people."

"I don't care. I want it back."

"I can't help you."

"Fine. I'll buy it back."

"It's already been sold."

I sat in the car near the dumpster outside my old apartment complex. A kid was riding his tricycle around the parking lot, no adult in sight. I remembered why I'd wanted a new life in the first place, no girlfriend, depressing apartment, dubious neighbors, dead end job. I had saved for years for the promise of a better life. Now I was back. Nothing had changed. I was the same person at heart, unhappy and dissatisfied.

I knocked on my old door. I used to never answer it, the only people who ever came by being Mormon missionaries, direct sales people and Jehovah's Witnesses. The man who answered was middle-aged, in a stained undershirt, graying moustache. Could he help me? I said I used to live here. Did I mind if I took a look around. Sure, he said.

The place hadn't changed. The TV was on. The kitchen smelled like a burnt TV dinner. Beyond the bathroom door I noticed a roll of toilet paper down to its last ply. The loud bass from the neighbor's reverberated through the wall.

"How do you like living here?" I said.

He shrugged. "It's O.K. Cheap. Can't complain."

"How much did you pay for this life?"

He narrowed his eyes at me. "If this is about my credit score, I can make the payments. Don't take this away from me."

"Relax. I'm not from the Life Center. This is my life you bought. I just want to know how much you paid for it."

When he told me I was surprised so many zeroes were attached to my name. Who would want this dump, this life, this meager existence? At the Life Center, the salesman had explained that mine was a starter life, a kind of temporary way station for someone seeking a better life. Once he had built enough equity, the current inhabitant of my life would move on, no doubt to something resembling more my own current situation. That is, if he was lucky. Some people never made it to the next stage. Some of them died, fell ill or racked up staggering debt before they could upgrade. Others complacently lingered in their mediocre lives, uninspired to reach the next plateau, happy with TV dinners, singlehood and apartment living.

I thanked the man for his time. As he showed me to the door, he asked me what, you know, the next stage was like.

"Pretty great," I said.

"I thought so."

Under the hazy light of dusk, the yard sprinklers created a misty vapor. Up and down the street, cars were nestled safely in their garage for the night. The curbside trash and recycling bins had been brought in. The houses glowed with an inviting warmth, promising pot roast and green beans. Through the kitchen window, Debra was chopping carrots and wiping her hands on her apron. Eric and Amanda had their heads bent over their textbooks at the kitchen table. The light turned purple, then black, a kind of enveloping twilight that covered me like a coat. It made me feel both safe and protected. I thought back to all the countless hopeless nights I spent dreaming of a scene like this one, of warmth, family, protection, safety and comfort. It was an illusory family sure, a collection of strangers gathered under the same roof, but over time I was confident I would begin to regard Amanda and Eric as my own children and Debra as my wife, and something akin to a real family would grow out of that love. I opened door and joined my new family.

Sustenance

Kathleen O'Toole

> *Which of you, if your child asked for bread,*
> *would give him a stone? Mt. 7:9*

I.

That first weekend in Intensive Care,
among the horror-movie particulars:
the ventilator hose lifts, like an alien's tentacle,
forcing breath through airways
choked with pneumonia.

Then beneath his elevated chin,
my father's southpaw script on the clipboard:
> *I love you.*
When do I get off this thing?
> *Sports page....*

———————

Quickly the doctors dictate
our choices: as soon as he's off,
he needs to know the risks of eating.

My sister riffs
on Durkheim's Law: all the new "choices" —
driftwood in technology's wake.

———————

> Meanwhile, we learn about the bacteria
> of pneumonia, like the varieties of crabgrass:
> this aspiration kind knows no weed killer;
> anaerobic bacteria have yet to meet
> their match in the antibiotic realm.

> And so he re-enters the world
> breathing but not eating. Fed, yes –
> first with IV fluids, and then via
> tube and pump: the nutrient-rich brew
> that would extend his life.

II.

Observe the lilies of the field —
the red geranium in the pot,
the swamp maple in the back yard —
they do not toil or reap,
yet they draw sustenance....

> Had anyone told me that this man,
> devotee of ice cream and meatloaf,
> black & white milkshakes, bacon & eggs
> over easy, would survive this loss —

Think of it: he is up,
able to walk and visit, pet
the cat and watch baseball.
But no hotdogs and beer, no
Tastykakes — no Holy Communion.

> So tiny gestures become sacraments:
> swabbing his dry mouth, applying cream
> to lips thinned from weeks without food
> or drink, delicate as when he and I nursed
> a downed nestling in a shoebox.

        Dew on a blade of grass, a few
        creamy blossoms on the gardenia,
            the rusty flash of a robin's wing
        at the window—can the other
           senses ever offset this loss ?

III.

Nearly a year for him to weigh
    this new existence. Against his wishes
we deny ourselves, try to relish with him:

sweet scent
from *that scraggly bush*—
white roses

        ship's clock chimes
        sparrow chatter in the fig tree
           last fruit

October sun
breeze shifting
the maple's shade

        dipping the swab
        in Communion wine —
        for New Years, ginger ale

Through it all, how he urges us: savor
all that sustains you, partake for me —
the flesh of new tomatoes, yeasty first bites
of cinnamon buns fresh from the oven,
hot coffee on the palate.

>   His Thanksgiving grace: bless us
>   O Lord, for these Thy gifts that THEY
>   are about to receive....

IV.

Impossible in the end
for us to deny all that bound us to him
    around a common table,
for him to accept the separation
    (only a drop of wine, never the host)
despite the blessing of time –

> *Do you know,* he asked
> after the speech therapist
> allowed him a spoonful
> of tapioca as a trial, *what it's like*
> *to taste after ten months?*

My brother still swears
    that on Ash Wednesday
Dad tilted the cup in the hands
    of the Eucharistic minister
and took a full gulp — *only say the Word,*
    and my soul shall be healed.

>   at the funeral home
>   his First Communion photograph
>   votive-lit

Twilight, Ardgroom
Kathleen O'Toole

Bumping along in the backseat of a van,
we pilgrims watch nubs of granite
strewn across Beara hillsides, see waves
crash over skelligs and stone beaches.
Scrubby tufts of grasses, a knobby yew
or two and palm fronds rustle as we pass.

At Ardgroom, the bog-soggy climb
across fields and over laddered fences
ascending to the ancient circle of stones.
Angelus hour. The rays transform
us into seven new strokes of shadow
moving among tines cast already
for three thousand years of days. Heedless
of us, a larger circle of ewes and lambs
bray their offering out. Incense altar,
smoke and scent rising from this odd
patch: pilgrims, stones, grasses, mud –
all earth. I finger the water-worn,
lichened stones one by one, lay
hands on the warmth of all nine
left standing.
              Now mind the spirit
of whoever hands erected this:
kil, cashel, timepiece, sacred space.
Here our elements strike ancestral flint.
Moon and star shine, bonfires, all
have lit this height, stirred air
that sanctifies wells, cairns,
Kenmare waters, ourselves —
touched, tethered, aglow.

Everything Is Breath

Eric Reymond

It was a situation for which my long years of studying had
 prepared me: I found a line that made no sense

I tried the obvious tricks first: writing until my hands
 cramped, sitting in dimly lit rooms

starving myself on tabletops, suspending myself thirty feet
off the ground

poring over minuscule print, outlasting cold winters only to
test myself against

a Mongol siege. When these did not produce results, I worked
myself as thin as the manuscript

cankered with worm holes and beaten with centuries of
light, and then I became the manuscript itself

and then the manuscript from which it had been copied and
so on

until I was the very beginning of literature and there I had
to transform again

and turn not only as thin as gas, but also as ebullient as
words --

I filled with laryngeals and uvulars, and slid across teeth
and lips, into a mouth and even down a throat

until I could go back further than tense or mood, into
something more primitive

where no matter how much I worked there was always
something more to feel

Summons
Paige Riehl

Meet me at the train tracks. Ride
your banana seat bike and tie
yellow ribbons to your handlebars. Bring
your voice for laughing. Wear nothing
on your head but the sun; we're riding
into yesterday. In the middle
of the city we'll coast by the tracks,
the abandoned grain mill, the brown brick
buildings with smashed windows: discarded
memories against the silver
and blue skyline. Remember being 16
in the back of someone's Buick?
Windows down and hair whipping,
singing songs and knowing seat
belts were for suckers? Remember
the sound the empty beer can made
as the wind sucked it from our hands? All
those cans disappearing into black,
in daytime glittering pieces
of discarded youth lying in ditches.
The snow has melted now.
Yesterday's garbage has risen
from the earth as if from hibernation—
dirty plastic bottles, beer cans, faded wrappers.
Leave the guilt and reproach at home. We're
alive. Bring garbage bags and thick
gloves. Together we will uncover
Arcadia.

Inheritance

Jane Satterfield

"If you and I are sitting here in a warm room having a nice talk, we have to ask ourselves how our own people survived. What did our people do at the time, that you and I came to be born? Anyone who had a field of cabbages or turnips put a guard on it to keep off the starving. We were those guards." —Nuala O'Faolin

To open her full freezer's unnerving—this Pandora's box of
    almost meals—
the poultry neatly skinned, trimmed & wrapped, an army
of baguette stumps saved for making gratin crumbs.

It's small price for seeing apocalypse at every corner,
this treasure trove layered deep as Troy
through which she'll have to dig.

But she can't seem to stop herself, buys
triple-berry medley by the bag
& grabs another, just in case.

When she thinks of famine roads,
fields blackened by blight, meals made
of nettles & weeds, carrion or grass,
a dose of unprocessed corn

which an official noted "was useful
as a ration of river sand," she's at
a loss for words. Watch her leap

from desk to kitchen,
the dough in suspended animation
rising under her floury hands.

Off-Hand Elegy
Jane Satterfield

    The death of Bruno Baskerville Walsh on 7/15/72 opens the first episode of the fourth season of HBO's Six Feet Under

    i.m. Scott Sanchez

In the dawn of that too-bright decade, that anglophile name
might have been a burden stoking his shyness,
a burden, the stately name meaning this boy's a scholar &
somehow not hip—.

*Family names no matter how bad can always
be forgiven* but a name too hard to live up to: isn't it little more
than a curse?

So then a dare, desire in the form of a girl, micro-skirted,
a dress to impress & the tab, the dose, the burden of time . . .

—Yes, bouquets & black armbands, *the red, white, and blue; wires
trip & boys
fragment in air; yes, dear host of willing distractions, dear party
without end*—

    What bloomed across the Atlantic in my grandfather's
    garden? From pictures I took, petunias & pinks . . .
    slow blitz of color under wan English sun after rain . . .
    in the blank
    field of the pocket diary I filled with scrawls nothing
    about fruited

cake for my eighth birthday, how the icing crackled like plaster
when cut, the Instamatic I carried along—7/15/72. . .

———————

Back on screen, the Haight-Ashbury glare, where time slowed to the moment
where the characters agree this high's *a chemical good*—

Cut to the rooftop leap, street noise, shocked passersby. Then cut
To a close-up of his name and the date.
Unclaimed ashes in a can.

———————

When Stephanie, flown out from South Central, sits across

the table, my heart's unhinged—there's his face in hers, the father she never
knew & upstairs the photo I own of cousins arranged at Santa's knee.
Her father—is he three?—looks already beaten, looks

past the camera to the junkie shotgun stare. While Stephanie talks
college I'm transported back to childhood's kitchen door
where whispers wove no narrative I knew: terrible temper, drugs,
that *tour. Alas, I am more oblivious, perhaps than you*—.

Plates are emptied, refilled, cabernet's swirled in the light.
We raise our glasses against the burden of time.

Returning from a journey, to what I'd long abandoned...
Mikhail Scherbakov

Издалека вернувшись туда, где не был долго,
взамен жилья и счастья найду пустые стены.
А в цветнике у дома за чугуном ажурным
увижу плоский камень, прочту на камне имя –
и, прислонясь к решётке, произнесу в смятенье:
«Ну как же так, Мария? Я ожидал иного.
Я думал, ты ещё раз спасёшь меня, как прежде.
Я был в тебе уверен. Я полагал, ты можешь всё…»

И шевельнётся камень, и покачнутся стебли.
И я услышу голос, который внятно молвит:
«Меняй дорогу, путник. Ты был не прав, как видишь.
Я не богиня вовсе, и не колдунья даже,
хоть и могу такое, чего никто не может:
могу не знать отрады, могу не быть любимой,
могу не ждать, не помнить, могу не петь, не плакать,
могу не жить на свете, но не могу не умирать…»

И снова всё умолкнет. Но вскоре тихим шагом
из дома выйдет некто, должно быть, местный сторож,
и спросит, чем обязан. И я солгу поспешно,
что перепутал адрес. И повернусь к воротам.
И засмеётся камень, и отшатнутся стебли.
И тихим шагом сторож пойдёт обратно к дому,
чтоб начертать отметку в своей учётной книге.
Так превратится в прочерк то, что когда-то было мной…

1991

Returning from a journey, to what I'd long abandoned...

Mikhail Scherbakov

Translated From the Russian by Ekaterina Chapiro

Returning from a journey to what I'd long abandoned,
Instead of joy and comfort, I'll find an empty dwelling.
And in the flowerbed, by the house's twisted railing,
I'll see a flattened gravestone, and read a name upon it -
And, leaning on the lattice, I will cry out in turmoil:
"How can this be, Maria? I didn't see this coming.
I thought that you would save me, the way you always had done.
I trusted in your powers. I really thought you knew it all..."

My words will move the gravestone. And blades of grass will rustle.
And I will hear a message, delivered very clearly:
"Change your direction, stranger. You had the wrong idea.
I'm not a mighty goddess, nor even an enchantress.
Though, I exist in ways that no human can imagine:
I can forego refreshment, I can refrain from loving,
I can cast off my memories, I can deny my sorrow,
I can be mute and absent - but I cannot refuse to die..."

And once again there's quiet. But soon, indistinct footsteps
Will creak along the pathway – must be the local keeper -
He'll ask me, what's the honour? And I will lie and tell him
That I mixed up the address. And turn to face the gateway.
And mirth will shake the gravestone. And blades of grass will tremble.
And with his muffled footsteps, the guard will cross the threshold,
To mark my name inside his long-cultivated guest book.
Thus turns to writing that, which - once upon a time - was me.

History of Ornament
Wendy Scott

I served beer from quarter-kegs
to graduate students of industrial administration
at my alma mater. Passing trays of sausage
on pastry in black pants/white shirt,
through room after room roped with origami,

thousands on thousands of paper cranes:
gilt, patterned, solid, batik-striped.
I was invisible. Except to one woman,
in a navy mini-dress who eyed me
up and down, entitled and speculative,

practicing for her own office lined with chair-rails,
her acre of desk. I was eyeing the birds:
first Christmas alone, first single-mother tree,
owning not one ornament. Drunk and glittering,
the students left—scorning wishes, the promise

of healing, good fortune. I took it all.
Outlasting that paycheck, dozens
of paper birds landed on these branches
from plastic bags gilled with gold, red, blue,
purple, flowered, checkered, silver, shining foil.

A Day Trip to Ellis Island

Peter Serchuk

The faces tell you, they knew why
they came: when the death you fear
and the life you live converge,
there is no door like a manic sea.
Here, on these muraled walls,
faces merge, hats trade heads,
histories blend. The more you stare,
the more you hear voices and clatter,
smell rotten food and sea scum.
In hallways long silent, ghosts question
ghosts in language raw and unfamiliar.
Questions, questions…
as if God himself was asking.
New arrivals stand in line for hours,
nervous, smiling, nodding at what
they don't understand, guessing at
answers they hope will ferry them
to solid ground. In this room,
gloved hands pry open mouths,
inspect teeth and scalps.
Behind that wall, other hands examine
places only night has seen.
The Norwegians look stout and ready,
not likely to be disappointed by the Dakotas.
The Irish, pale, but eager to hit the streets.
And the Jews, eyes bloodshot with history,
wait for passports to promised lands.

Any dog will bite
Leona Sevick

Out my kitchen window I see
my son, sitting still on the bank
behind our house. His shoulders
curl forward like a question
mark as he props his elbows
on his knees. The gun,
which looks to me like any real gun,
shoots small plastic pellets
from an orange tip. He stares
unblinking through the sights
arranged on the barrel,
the pink tip of his tongue
exploring his upper lip.
He squeezes the trigger,
nailing the paper target twenty
yards away. Over and over
he reloads and fires, making
tiny adjustments that improve
his aim. I can almost feel
the clicking of good gears
in his eleven-year-old head,
can almost smell the concentration
in his boy's fingers. From here
I can only see the side
of his face, shining with triumph
and maybe something more.
"Any dog will bite," is one of those
things my father says
from time to time. I know

he means to teach me lessons
until they sink in, like the teeth
of that snapping mongrel he sees
in his head, the dog a stand-in
for everything he fears or thinks I should.

Zoonosis

Leona Sevick

There is no end to the dangers animals pose.
Microscopic deer ticks have the indecency
to leave behind swollen joints, fever

and fatigue after sucking our blood.
Neglected dogs and ordinary raccoons
become bewildered malcontents,

appearing in strange habitats, snapping
at us with their foaming jaws.
And those innocent cows, munching

away in patty-smeared fields, contaminate
our boots and somehow cause our brains to swell.
Instead, what if we passed our crippling

maladies to our animal friends?
When we stroke their backs and scratch
behind their ears, feeling along the tender

depressions in their skulls, what if we infested
them with anxieties, with depression inked in
deepest blue? Suppose we splashed our

traumatic memories in Technicolor across
their innocent brains, paralyzing their senses?
What if, unwittingly, we infected an army

of mosquitoes with our control issues?
Swarming in unison, they would look for ways
to call the shots for every living thing.

Imagine the damage that we'd do.

Incisor

Spencer Smith

Grandpa grins crookedly and there it is
like a scorched kernel of corn,
partially turned and leaning slightly to the left
to rest wearily on the shoulder
of an ivory canine in distress.

On days when I am not with him
it is difficult to bring to mind his face—
the icewater eyes, brambled brow,
bold tan nose and stubbled cheeks and jawline;
his features merely frame the tooth.

Someone says the word brown
and it pings at me insistently. I imagine it
carving its way down through a doughnut,
squashing more than cutting, finally
coming to rest on its alter ego below.

I ask him one day in unexpected blurt
why he doesn't just get it fixed.
It can't be that much money, I insist.
He only chuckles hoarsely, pats my arm,
says it doesn't bother him. But it bothers me.

I try to sleep but cringe at the indelible image,
wondering if it tastes like what it looks like,
wondering how I could face the TV each day
with those unfairly beautiful people smiling,
teeth white as peppermint, white as plastic.

Classical Electrodynamics
(for J.D. Jackson)

Peter P. Sordillo

It was the origin of the numbers he would not explain:
Equations, fragments of shadows still clinging
To a garden wall. None of us could understand
Why curled letters, figures on a page,
Breed pools of green water where the lights diverge,
How processions of these symbols could engender
Amber and lodestone, and sunset in the garden,
Why what begins in truth must end in longing.

Snow beats hard against the window now. Light
Blazes in the Russian student's eyes,
And her waving hand touches all of space,
For the air is fire, whose arms stretch everywhere
And forever. I must abandon
Desires that end for desires that do not.

Father Frequencies
(Knicks 88 Bulls 87: Game 5, Semi-Conference Finals, 1994)

Dario Sulzman

Your father wakes you in the night.
    He wakes you in the bed where he sleeps
when you're not there. He wakes you
    to your own sweat, to dry darkness
and fibrous radio static. Listen, he says.
    He wakes you now, primetime-past-bedtime,
seven seconds left, Knicks down by one.
    Mike Breen's coiled voice clears space
on a lisping bandwidth--
    Knicks inbound on the left hand side.

He wakes you for dewy golf dates and long car rides.
He wakes you in tents and hotel rooms. He wakes you
with overeager phone calls on Sunday mornings when
you're hung over. He has trouble sleeping.
    He stands in shadows
        Starks is doubled
    arms crossed
        throws it to Davis
    holding something in.

Maybe he's cold. He wears tattered long
    underwear and sleeps in the living room.
Davis is *wide open*. Back rims the three
    but he's fouled, *fouled by Pippen.*
You can't see your father's face
    but his head bobs like a Hasid in prayer.

He wakes you with grease-black fingers
    with a saw clearing its throat on a fresh board.
He yells at you to wake up and *listen*
    because you've cut the copper lines wrong
and he's too busy to show you again.

He wakes you to say he's leaving.
You awaken to see he's come back.
He wakes you as fathers wake sons
footsteps close like basketballs
announcing their pressured hearts
through dreams and darkness.

Adamless Eden
Kelly M. Sylvester

Transplanted young women
uprooted from the streets *to follow the plow*

soiled in East Meadow estate, farmerettes
at the 1911 Brookholt School of Agriculture for Women

woke before the golden sun rises,
toiled to turn 2,000 acres into gold—

these Eves' dressed in Alva's designer divided skirts
fed, housed, paid an allowance to hoe land…

a year of tutelage elapses,
crops still struggling for life;

not one of the twenty farmerettes
blossomed into a true farm-hand;

no-post graduates among the lot
hardly could learn to milk or *grow flowers;*

Alva's failed school weeds women from acres
first, and only, farmerettes fallen from grace.

Note: This poem is based on the research of Alva Smith Vanderbilt Belmont.

Hurricane Isabel September 12
Savannah Thorne

The rain
is the marrow
in the bones of the house.
Storms
are letters
handwritten in water.
I sleep surging
in the water of dreams.
What drops
drops like apples
through cold green depths
to childhood, to memory,
to whatever is unearthed
on murky bottoms
past the vanishing point:
driftwood bones,
the white of a rope
gleaming dully.
I had thought
earth was cold.
But this is the earth's graveyard,
where even things refused
go to die.

Hurricane Isabel September 19
Savannah Thorne

A skein of white snow cuts
Barer than January.
Each month: a suffering, a triumph.
How tired
We've become, like fetching
Cold water from a pit with a spoon.
Pinning the long horizon with ice.
The tingle of numbness
Is a warning:
There are small dark angels in our fingertips.
The silence of the soul
Becomes god
Escaping clean out
Like a migration
To warmer climes.
Birds scatter through
The bell-bright curve of light. We can last,
We believe, beyond this.
The earthy grit of life;
Measured this deep, this black.

Hurricane Isabel September 21
Savannah Thorne

Mine are the denizens of frogspawn.
Mine, the lily of the valley and the
Endless grasses. Mine, the days
You have nothing to learn from
But how to listen. There—
The spanning wings
Of hummingbirds awreck
In a sea of broken wood. There—the slabbed lot
Bamboozled with cracks,
Snowflakes hung
Over a wind-wracked world.
Though memories roll in my mouth
I can only tell you
Of the moist, brackish, burrowing
That becomes what you are.
I can only hold out my hands
And tell you: this is what you have
To build from.

21 Days
Tina Tocco

When Grandma told the story, they were on the boat from Naples for 21 days. They ate from the captain's garbage. They drank from the Atlantic. Her little sister's dress was so short, she did not dare stand up in it. For 21 days.

Grandma told this story when we asked for a nickel for a soda, a dime for an ice cream. When we complained that the Parker girls across the street all got new shoes, and when we had eaten bread sopped in oil for 10 meals straight. She used it to explain why our pants were either cuffed or too tight in the crotch, why Mom had to spend nights at the curtain factory. Why Grandpa hit. Why they never liked Dad at any of his jobs.

We did not tell Grandma that, at PS 4, they taught us how a boat from Naples to America did not take 21 days. Or that Uncle Paulie, on his second bottle one Thanksgiving, told us that nothing ever tasted as sweet as wine at the captain's table. Or that salt water kills you. And we did not tell Grandma how, when her cancer got bad, we started sorting through her things. And how the pictures were there. Hundreds. And hundreds. Grandma, tiny, in a silk hat. Her father in pin-straight slacks. A brick house so big, it did not fit in the frame. Ladies in long dresses, dancing, looking like they'd never sit down.

Promised Land
Tina Tocco

Like me, Granddad Mose never knew his momma. He overheard his daddy tell the story once, about how when he was being born, his momma woke up twice and asked if it was over. At dusk, his daddy had his supper and went to the outhouse, as he was inclined to do, and when he came back in for his pie, the lady there — a midwife, Granddad supposed — said she'd asked again. At some point, she stopped asking.

When he sensed the sunrise, my great-granddaddy rose from the hayloft to tend the cows and the horses, and finally collect the eggs. Back at the house, the lady told him, "She's gone to the Promised Land."

My momma went to the Promised Land, too. It said so on the postcard, above the trees. I didn't know they were trees. They had long sharp things sticking out of them. Granddad Mose said they were called cactuses. He said they lived in the harshest places on earth, with no water, yet they brimmed cool and sweet on the inside. He said thirsty animals lunged at them, and learned their lesson. He said, even though you couldn't see it in the postcard, cactuses bloomed the most beautiful flowers — pink like the bubblegum daddy used to bring me, and blood red.

I read the postcard again. I could read all the words now. It said, in letters bigger than mine, "Baby girl, miss you bunches. The little ones want to meet their big sis. Can't write no more. No room."

Girl

LaToya Watkins

    I drunk a whole cup of castor oil when Black ain't come see me last Thursday night. Two months without hearing from him was enough for me. I ain't want to call him without it being important though. I knowed he was with her, smiling like me and Chase and the baby cooking inside me ain't even exist. Like we don't live in Parkway Village projects, and like he didn't never come smoke with me while she teaching first graders how to read.

    I drunk the castor oil to make the baby come early, but now they say he fighting for his life. Say he was in distress and ain't get enough oxygen. And on top of all that, Black still ain't come when I called. He finished his night with his wife and come handing me leftover time while I pushed out his second son.

    This his first time seeing the baby since I had him Friday morning. He ain't sitting close to me rubbing my back the way he did when we was in the new natal ICU with Chase. He standing over the cubator with his eyes closed like he praying or something. Like the baby the star, and I ain't nothing. I guess that's what it look like the way they got the light beaming down on him and his eyes all covered up.

    A white couple on the other side of the room. The man standing over the woman, and she holding one of they three new babies. The baby got a I.V. in its head and a tube through its nose, but the woman rocking the chair like it's normal. The man rubbing her head and smiling. I want me and Black to be like them.

    "I think he gone be all right," I say. I want him to nod and let me know he know I'm here, but he don't. He keep his eyes closed and start humming.

Thursday wasn't the first time I drunk castor oil to make Black come. I drunk it with the first baby, Chase, to get his attention—to get him to come back home to me. But with Chase I was too too early. Twenty-five weeks is all I had gave him to grow. He fought to live the whole time he was in Methodist, but he made it out alive. They put a metal plate in his head cause his little skull part wasn't strong enough to hold his little bitty brain. Now his head shaped like a Frisbee, and his eyes won't sit in his head the way normal folks' do. They cross all the time. When I finally brought him home he was six months, but he looked like a newborn. He three now, but he look like he one. He can't walk, but he get around real good on his hands and knees. Black look at him like he pitiful. I guess he kind of is. Always sitting there slobbering and talking baby talk. Can't even see if I don't put on them baby bifocals the doctor say he need to wear. Black don't know bout the castor oil, and he surely don't know I named Chase after how I was chasing after him. He don't even know the boy is going blind and dying slow.

"This has been a mistake, Mahogany," Black say, finally opening his eyes. "All of this is my fault. I shouldn't have been there...ever." It make me kind of nervous that he calling me by my whole name like he don't know me down to my panties.

"It's okay, Black," I say. "If he ain't good, we can try again. We can do it till we get it right."

He finally turn to look at me and his face confuse me. He handsome. His fresh haircut and trimmed beard hiding the few gray hairs I'm used to seeing. His clothes look new, and I ain't used to seeing that either. I ain't gone fuss about it. I want to ask him why he done that though. Go get new clothes and a haircut without Chase, but I ain't gone fuss. He rub his hand over his head and sigh real loud like he tired or something. I want to say something to him, but he don't feel like the same person I smoked with before.

"You got something?" I whisper. "I ain't had nothing since you made me quit. I ain't pregnant no more." That make me smile. We can get high together again. I ain't got to hide it from him no more. He don't get mad when I get high without his babies in my stomach.

Me and Black got more in common than him and his wife. She think she all fancy and smart, but me, I get down and dirty with my man. She won't let him get high in her house. I let him do what he want in mine. She holy, but he don't have to deal with that kind of mess from me. But the main way we common is we can have babies. His wife ain't gave him no baby in the ten years they been married.

He shake his head. "I will never have that for you again, Mahogany. Never," he say, and spit spray out his mouth.

I don't know what to say. Don't know if he for real or just hurting about the new baby. I kind of want to turn the light on and brighten up the room—see his eyes, but the babies in here is sleep and sick and dying and I ain't gone mess with that.

Black was happy when I got pregnant with Chase. His high eyes opened bout as wide as he could get them. Said he was too close to forty not to have no son. Was hurting cause him and his wife had been trying so long. He got scared when the doctor got to talking bout something being wrong with my cervix and put me on bed rest. I don't know if I could have carried Chase the whole time, but my friend-girl told me I could take some castor oil to make him come early if I was ever tired of being pregnant.

I kind of don't know why he ain't left his wife. She ain't all woman since she ain't gave him what I done did twice. He don't come from Parkway Village like me, but we from the same place. East Lubbock. We know the flat plains, red dirt, and the funk of cow shit. We both know what being poor like too. Me more than him, but she don't know at all. Her folks come from Atlanta. He met her up there in when he was in college. I know its fancy down there. He talk bout the tall buildings and black folks worth something. He talk bout whole families like the one his wife come from. Say she come from a home with a momma and a daddy and ain't nobody do drugs.

Me, I live the same projects I was born in. I ain't never been out of West Texas, but I been out of Lubbock plenty of times. Done seen what the world like outside the East side. That make me better than my momma. She joined to East Lubbock in her heart. Been a stone junky for twenty years. And I don't even know who my daddy is. That's like Chase, only I saved his daddy for him. He just too slow to know his daddy when he see him. But if this one make it, he gone be whole, and me and him and Black gone be a family like the ones in Atlanta.

"You hear me, baby? Hear what I said? That one gone be good. This one gon—"

"I can't do this with you anymore, Mahogany. You've lost yourself, little girl," he say real quiet, turning around to look at me. He so beautiful and neat and look like he smell like something fresh to smoke. "That's why they keep coming like this…" he say, stretching his hand out toward the baby. He start crying, and I stand up really quick. I go toward him and he shake his hand. "They keep coming here damaged because I touched what I shouldn't have. I was blessed with football and Mattie and getting out of this place, but I've wronged Him." He wave his hand back-and-forth between me and him. "This is wrong."

And I'm scared. He ain't brought up football and how he lost it since the beginning of us. The drugs help keep that pain away. I'm scared cause I know something—somebody—done scratched it out of his head.

"Our boys is miracles, baby. These your only sons—your only kids. I love you, Black. Look at me. It's Hoggy. I lo—"

"Shh," the white woman with baby say, putting her fingers her lips like I'm five. I nod at her and try to smile. I look at her for a while. She holding that baby like she ain't gone never let go. Like even if it die in her arms she ain't gone let go. If my momma had been white with a husband that rub her back, maybe she wouldn't have never let me go. Maybe she wouldn't have ran to drugs. Maybe I wouldn't have followed her.

Looking at the white momma make me wish I was white. Wish I could make my man come home without drinking castor oil.

I look back at Black. He sticking his hands through the incubator, rubbing the baby's tiny head. "That night—that day we saw you at KWIK-O, that was Mattie's first day on the East side. She only agreed to move here to make me feel like a man." He shake his head and close his eyes. He still rubbing the baby head, but it look like he dreaming.

I remember the day he talking about. I was hanging out at the KWIK-O Car Wash—I always hanged out there. On Friday nights, the old abandoned washing stalls and empty vacuum spaces used to be filled up with everybody worth something from or on the East side. Black and his wife pulled up at the convenience store next to KWIK-O like a accident. Some of the ballers at the wash knowed him from when he was one of us—fore Atlanta—fore football—when he got out to go in the store. They called him over and that's when I heard about him being some professional football player. I wasn't but eighteen back then. Still young and lost. I was trying to be seen by him—by any baller. Trying to be found and in love.

He brought his wife over with him. She was a pretty, in a old, homely kind of way, but she wasn't good enough to have no footballer like Black. She was a yellow-skinned woman with a short afro. No tight clothes, no pushed up titties to hold his eyes, no nothing. She ain't belong at KIWK-O. She ain't belong on the East side. And after that night, she ain't never come back east of the loop no more. I walked the lot hard that night cause I wanted him to see what a real woman looked like. I felt like something big when he pulled up the next week without his wife in the car and smiled at me. It didn't even bother me when he called me over and asked me where Don Juan was. I knew what he was looking for when he asked about Don, but I ain't care. I acted like I was down even though I hadn't never smoked nothing but weed before. We fell in love that night with our eyes all lazy. That was four years ago and I still love him like that first night.

"After my injury, I died," he say. "I died and wanted to bring her to hell with me. Told her the only thing that would ever make me happy would be coaching at Tech," he say. He open his eyes and open his palm over the baby's plum-sized head. He hold his hand over the head without touching it. Look like he concentrating on a crystal ball or something. "They hired me. Injury and all. That wasn't enough for me. I was ungrateful and I threw it all away."

"We got a family," I say. He shake his head.

"No, Mahogany. This has been a mistake." And this time I shake my head.

"How can this be wrong?" I ask, walking over to the incubator. "This a child of…," I stop. I look at the too-little baby. When he cried after I had him, he sounded like a squealing rat. His head so little. His body so little. Bigger than Chase's was, but still little. I look at Black and feel my lips shaking.

"It's over, Mahogany. I'm sorry I brought you into this," he say. I wonder if this mean he gone take Chase with him the next time he get a haircut or go shopping. I wonder if he gone come around more, and maybe next time I won't have to drink castor oil. I wonder if he gone leave her.

"It's okay, Black." I stand close to him, but I don't touch him.

"No," he shake his head and his lips start to shake like mine. "God'll never forgive me for what I've done to you—to Mattie." He take his hands out of the cubator and step away from me.

"Why you keep saying her name?" I ask in a whisper, looking at the woman with the three babies.

"When he can come home, he's coming with me. With us," he say.

I don't know what to say. I can't believe this is happening. I want to do a snakey dance like I seen somebody do at church a long time ago. I knowed one day he was gone come home with us, but I wasn't expecting it for real.

"I talked to Mattie—came clean about everything. She's hurting, but she understands that you need help. Knows what it takes. She loved me clean." He nod his head like he thinking bout something. "I-I'll get Chase, too," he say like he don't want to. "We'll take them both," he say.

"Huh?" I say. My voice done went hoarse, but it ain't coming out in no whisper. Now I understand he ain't talking bout coming home with us. He talking bout taking my gifts to her. "What you talking bout, Black? Taking them? Leaving me? Why you want to leave me?" I feel my breathing speed up. I need something in my system before I explode. I look at the door and think bout where Don Juan at.

"Shh," the rocking woman say.

"They say you got a year to clean up, Mahogany," Black say. "We'll take good care of them until you can get it together. If you can't—"

"Leave me? You want to leave me?" I ask as loud as I can. The woman shush me again and I look at her real hard and mad. I think about shutting my mouth and all the times I done kept it closed in my life. I think bout grandmomma fore she died and left me with momma. How I used to pray for momma to get clean and stop letting her men friends touch my titties. I think bout how I waited quiet for Black to leave his wife and come home to me. I think bout how loud castor oil speak and what it say. "Shush yourself, bitch. I'm a momma just like you—a woman. You can't shush nobody," I say after a while.

"Mahogany, you should leave," Black say. He got surprise in his eyes and I ain't never seen them open so big. "Don't do this here."

"Yes, you should leave," the woman's man say, coming to where me and Black standing. "I'm getting a nurse or security."

"Please, sir," Black say, holding his hand out as the man try to pass us. He headed for the nurse station, and I don't care. I ain't leaving without my man. I ain't leaving without a fight. "She's leaving, sir," Black say. "Just let me get her out of here. You're right, she shouldn't be here." He take his other hand out of the cubator, and I smile because he reaching for me like he gone hold me or something.

But he don't. He don't even touch me. He lean in close to me and whisper, "Leave, Mahogany. I can't help you if you're in jail."

The white man standing there like he waiting on my next move. Like he want to see if I'm gone leave and make the whole place safe. I look from him to Black, and I don't see Black no more. I see a clean stranger without raggedy gray hairs and lazy eyes. He ain't my Black at all. And I wonder what I am without him.

"I ain't knowed no pipe without you," I say, and I can hear crying in my voice. "I ain't knowed none of the stuff I know now." I hold out my hands like I'm Jesus. "What you expect me to do now, Black?"

The white man walk back over to his wife when I start crying soft and rubbing my nose. Black go back and put his hands in the cubator. And I stand there until my breathing get too heavy, and I know I need something in my system to stop me from exploding.

Between Two Poles

Colleen Wells

Screw with your meds. You haven't had an episode in six years and not one in fourteen more before that, so by all means be cavalier with your Abilify.

Begin to notice that life is good. While your sons are in school you write ten pages a day before going to enjoy your work in a diner. Look for another job anyway, like a PR position at a cat shelter. Enjoy the mild weather in central Tennessee. Hear music as if it were written for you.

Because life is so awesome, you feel more spiritual. Research women of the Bible. Identify with the sinners. Read your sons' old toddler Bible and become fixated on Jonah.

Start staying up late. Write an essay about President Obama, cats and the television series CSI. Tie the threads together connecting them all in an essay while your neurotransmitters are flying so quickly they spark. Send that essay out to all your friends and family.

Go to the bookstore, buy five copies of the children's anthology from the 70s, Free to Be, You and Me, purchase more religious books and a novel you believe a former professor wrote about you under a pen name. E-mail the professor, ask him if he ever wrote under a pen name.

Show your husband the ten page single-spaced document of ideas to give the director of the cat shelter. Promise him you're fine when he looks at you with concern. While you're on the topic of cats, tell him the answer to the overpopulation problem is to take them to prisoners where they'll help with the inmates' rehabilitation the way dogs sometimes do. Go to the doctor to prove you are ok. Let him and your husband talk privately about how prophetic you are. They can't even begin to understand what makes you tick. Take the medication your husband gives you. Get a painful rash from it. Go back to the doctor. Tell him you don't like the décor in his office.

Become convinced there are bombs in the TV.

Become certain your husband is giving you arsenic along with your meds. He has taken away your cell phone and computer so you can't tell anyone. Take comfort when you hear the hum of airplanes overhead while you sit on the back porch. You're certain they are full of your friends coming to save you.

Discover empty Gatorade bottles and candy wrappers in your son's closet, become convinced the professor who wrote about you is living there. Give bandanas and postcards to your aunt who has come to help. Tell her they're for him.

Be forced to go to the hospital. In the elevator mention to the escort she has a lot of arm waddle. Hear the familiar ominous click of the locked doors behind you.

Don't remember anything about the night except for the nurse who sat by your bed and how you were scared she'd leave you to die. In the morning you can barely walk and hold on to the walls of the hallway while crying out for coffee.

Believe the old man on the couch is a reincarnated version of your husband. Days later when the meds start working realize you were wrong. Notice he isn't wearing anything under his hospital gown. Look away.

Recognize that the other patients are worse off than you. They are mentally ill and homeless. Or mentally ill and addicted to meth. You are just mentally ill.

At home you are back on e-mail. You cringe at what's in your sent box. Discover that you sent a poem about your menstrual cycle to your sons' soccer coach. Notice how many messages you sent to your college professor. Attempt to e-mail him an apology. Discover he's blocked his account from getting your messages. Notice the light from the computer hurts your eyes. Shut it off. While you sit there, feel the creep of a nagging headache as your body adjusts to going off the nicotine patch they gave you in the hospital.

Realize there are other adjustments to make. It is clear your sons look to your husband for everything now. Let them because you don't know how to regain your footing as a person, let alone as a parent.

Take comfort in the fact the dogs still need you.

Try getting your job back from the couple who own the diner. He says you're welcome to return to work. She says things have slowed down and they don't need the help.

The memories start flooding back to you about how you thought you were a prophet and even prepared a speech for your guest spot at the church. You see sticky goo in the mailbox and recall how you poured green tea inside so you could christen it in preparation for your letter of acceptance from a book publisher. Find other clues to your madness such as the random objects in the bushes out front—your 1966 U. S. mint coins—a gift from your grandfather when he was alive, his rosary and tortoise shell square-dancing bolo, which you inherited when he died.

As you change clothes notice how much weight you lost while you were manic.

Feel alone. Feel nothing. Call one of the patients you made friends with in the hospital. She tells you how abusive her boyfriend is, how he threw all her shit in the street and locked her out. Try to commiserate about how your husband locked the gate to the back yard to keep you on the property. But realize the difference. One man was trying to hurt, another help.

Slowly sink into the depression you knew would come. Sit on the back porch chain-smoking. Call your friends and have nothing to say. Try making spaghetti for the family in an effort to contribute. Feel the weight of fatigue set in after filling the pot with water. Go back to the porch and wrap a blanket around your shoulders because you feel old. Hear the laughter of neighborhood children through the trees. Wonder if you'll ever laugh again.

Get your meds adjusted. Wait. Discover one of them is making a twitching feeling up and down your legs like you've got bugs crawling inside your skin. Note the dark tint of your urine. Tell your doctor, who tinkers with your pharmaceutical cocktail again. Become more skeptical of psychiatry, but know there's something to it, because if you hadn't messed up your meds in the first place, this wouldn't have happened.

See a therapist. Try to believe her when she says you won't always feel this way. Wait some more.

Realize once again you are bipolar, your moods swing between two poles.

When you finally do balance out, notice how you are grateful for the big picture. You are mentally ill, but not homeless. You are mentally ill but not on meth. You are mentally ill, but not abused.

Note that while life isn't perfect, and you'll never solve the feral cat problem with delusional thinking, you do what you can do.

Make chocolate chip cookies for your kids. See how much they like them. See how resilient and forgiving they are. See how resilient you are.

Forgive yourself.

Call It a Night
by Kathleen Wheaton

"Who goes out on New Year's night?" Leda says.

"We're not tired," her children say. They are five-ten, six feet. They're going back to college in two days.

"But I have an important interview tomorrow and I need my sleep," Leda says.

It's eleven-thirty p.m. and Big and Little are dressed to go out: clean flannel shirts, Old Spice deodorant. The gray sweats they've worn since rising at noon are coiled on the floor like the shed skins of snakes. "Can't you just put on your dinosaur pajamas and call it a night?" she says.

They laugh then and kiss her because life without her is in sight.

"You sleep fine when they're away at school," her husband, Joe, says. "Why not when they're home?"

"I'm not taking questions from reporters," Leda says, and pulls the covers over her head. Usually, she can doze for a couple of hours before being jolted awake at two by depleted hormones and worry.

That was how it was when the boys were a toddler and a newborn. They were living in a village in Mexico then, during a peasant uprising, under a volcano. The snowy peak shone blue in the moonlight as she wore a path on the carpet with Little, who was screaming with colic. "Take him back to his real home on that mountain," Big sobbed as he trailed along behind her, clutching the hem of her nightgown.

"This is his real home, sweetie. Don't you remember when we drove to the hospital in Cuernavaca?" It had been a harrowing trip, with police roadblocks and amniotic fluid leaking all over the car.

"Take him back to the hospital," Big wailed, as the baby wept. She rocked them in the hammock on the veranda, humming Sweet Baby James over and over again. The moon shimmered through the trees and then faded, like an apparition.

At breakfast, only Leda seemed to remember what the night had been like. Three tousled blond heads greeted her, three sunny smiles.

"God, those look like bruises under your eyes," Joe said. "Tonight, it's my turn to get up with them."

But before bedtime, army trucks had rolled into the jungle to the south, and away he went to cover the story. At his preschool, Big drew dead campesinos in pools of red. He'd heard his parents talking when they'd thought he was asleep.

Eighteen years later, in the Maryland suburbs, Little is the biggest. Leda had warned Big that this might happen, after he'd pinched his baby brother. Big had turned in his car seat and regarded Little dispassionately. "I'll always be bigger than him--that's how it works."

How it works is that Little still defers to his shorter, smaller brother, and Leda still believes that this 170-pound man needs her protection.

On New Year's Eve, for example, she'd driven Little and his two high school friends, Liban and James, to a party because she hadn't wanted them driving.

But the party turned out to have been cancelled. "I can have some people over to my house--my mom's got a shift at work tonight," Liban said. "It's totally fine with her," he assured Leda.

"Really," Leda said. She hasn't met Liban's mother, who works insane hours at a hospital, but she likes her. Because their names are similar, all through high school Leda would get texts meant for Liban saying, Get home this minute! You're in trouble!

James' mother she doesn't like. "If they're going to drink, they might as well do it in my basement," she'd once told Leda, in her sweet Southern voice, her pretty little face framed with chestnut curls.

"So other people's kids can drive home drunk?" Leda had fumed to Joe. "I wanted to strangle her."

"I believe you," he'd said.

Liban directed her to his house, which looked somehow different at night. Through the windshield she watched the three boys trying doors and windows, trampling the azaleas. But they weren't her azaleas. They got back in the car.

"She said she'd leave the garage door unlocked, but she forgot," Liban said.

"You don't have a key to your house?" Leda said. "Wait. Is this your house?"

"It's like my house. They're super-close friends."

Leda drove them back to her neighborhood, the bass thumping. Everyone was driving with slow, balletic, exaggerated courtesy. Police were everywhere. It was probably the safest night of the year to be on the road. That is what Joe had said. He was waiting for her at home with Champagne.

"What if it turns midnight and we're stuck in this car with my mom?" Little said mournfully.

Leda pulled over. "You're free to get out and walk."

"Sorry, sorry, I didn't mean it like that. We just have to think a sec." Then, placating, "What are you and Dad doing tonight?"

"I don't know," she said, because the passions of the old are appalling to the young. "Playing Scrabble, maybe."

"That's so lame." The boys laughed and cheered up.

"Why don't we go to Grace's?" Little said. "We could get out and walk there."

"I'll call Mario," James said. "He knows her."

"Is it a good idea to go to the party of a girl you don't know?" Leda said.

"I know her really well," Little said. "I just don't have her phone number."

After Scrabble and Champagne, Joe slumbered as Leda tossed, dry-mouthed and headachy. Distant sirens made her go rigid, lobster-claw hands clutching the duvet. She tried relaxing, starting with her feet, her brain skittering frantically up and down her body like a cockroach. At four the kitchen door slammed; once, twice. The voices of Big and Little. Happy New Year, she whispered, to whatever power had brought them safely home.

The next night, New Year's night, Leda awakens and counts backward from a hundred. Then from two hundred. Then to and from a hundred in Spanish. More alert than ever, she listens to the sighing of the wind in the silver maples, the ghostly bark of a fox.
    At three-ten the boys arrive. Cupboards open and close, the microwave fires up. The kitchen seems to be filling with people--word must be out on Twitter that Leda stocked up on Easy Mac. The screen porch door bangs, over and over and over. Among the hubbub of voices, at least one girl's. Good. From Leda's vantage point, girls are fabulous. Such developed prefrontal cortexes. Mothers of girls tell her this is a problem: they remember everything you say and fling it back in your face.
    Of all the unapproved teen activities, sex always seemed to Leda the best option. Though no sooner is this thought formed than she sees a row of mean-girl faces with blow-dried 70's hair, mouthing, You would, slut.
    Safe sex, of course. When Big brought home a permission slip to see a condom video in eighth grade, she was shocked: What parent in her right mind would say no to this? She turned the sheet over. "Where can I sign you up for extra help?"
    "Not funny, Mom."

Even now, they think she's kidding when she's dead serious.

She drifts in and out of consciousness, an unmoored boat. At a quarter to five, a clatter of feet on the stairs. She pulls on her robe and there's Little on the stair landing, white-faced, red trickling from one corner of his mouth.

"What on earth?"

He assumes as much nonchalance as a bleeding person can. "Nothing."

"But there's blood coming out of your mouth."

He swipes at it. "It's dried, mostly. And I'm really tired."

He goes into his room and shuts the door. A blue light shines from underneath. It's nearly morning, but he's got to say goodnight to his 844 Facebook friends.

Three hours later, Joe, dressed for work, brings her a mug of tea. "They're both safe in their beds--I checked," he says. "You see? If we just go to sleep and don't worry, they make it home fine."

On the screen porch, five cigarette lighters in a circle, a fairy ring. Big appears at eleven, looking windblown and rosy as if he'd spent the morning hours hiking in the Alps. Leda greets him, then whacks the front page of the Post. "It says here that marijuana is still illegal in Maryland."

Big stretches, smiles. "Our friends know you don't like it. That's why they sat out in the cold." His gaze softens as he looks back across the years from twenty to high school. "Some of them are even still scared of you."

Leda's doing a series of interviews for a book on what makes a successful marriage, but so far only one man has answered her query. His description of himself was promisingly candid, though; even literary: sandy-haired, balding, burly, and she finds him easily in the cafe where they agreed to meet.

Her description of herself hasn't changed in twenty-five years, though she has: blondish hair, glasses.

"Leda? Mark." Mark is the pseudonym he's chosen.

He's drinking a glass of wine. She orders tea, takes out her pen and notebook.

"Ah, the memories," he says.

"My kids say I'm the most analog person they know."

"No, I mean I used to be a journalist," Mark says. "I was on the Metro desk of the Sun in the eighties, so you can imagine how crazy. And I had this crazy Latina wife."

"Careful," she says. "My younger son was born in Mexico."

"Adopted? That's terrific. I so admire people who do that."

"Actually, he's--" she stops. This is an interview, not a conversation. She nods and smiles.

"My wife was Venezuelan. Gorgeous. She thought she had it made, marrying a gringo. She quit her job and didn't lift a finger around the house. She'd leave her dirty dishes in the sink, like that was doing the dishes. So one night, for a joke, I bring all her plates and leave them by her side of the bed. She gets up, knocks over a glass and cuts her foot. Suddenly she's heaving stuff at me. I know that kind of thing seemed funny on I Love Lucy, but I ended up in the ER with fourteen stitches." He inclines his head and runs a finger across a thin white scar along his jawline.

"Wow, I can see it, even in this light," Leda says, while thinking, I'd have cut your throat, pal. It's a lying, sordid profession, journalism. "So would you say that this crisis strengthened your marriage?"

"Well, she went back to Venezuela. But I got smarter about women. My second wife is low-maintenance, ladylike, a Virginian. She's devoted to our son."

Now Leda's studying him, squinting. He seems familiar. Or maybe all fatuous expressions look alike. "So is a woman being low-maintenance key to a successful marriage, in your opinion?"

He nods encouragingly, as to a struggling pupil. "Money is also key, though most people won't admit that. The second smartest thing I did was quit the paper because you can't raise a family on a journalist's salary."

Leda sips her tea, which is now cold. "Did you know Joe Murphy when you were at the Sun?" she says, though she knows she shouldn't.

"Oh, sure," Mark says. "Colleague of yours? Journalism was like his religion. Though talk about your crazy women."

"Really?" Her hand shakes a little as she puts down her cup.

"He was living with this gal and one day she up and leaves. Moves to Boston to become a poet, like nothing rhymes in Baltimore. Murphy was traumatized. Guy went from being the Metro desk party animal to a total workaholic. It was sad."

"Thank you." Leda closes her notebook. "I think I have what I need."

He hands the waiter his credit card, waving her proffered card aside. "Is it too late for this to be off the record?"

"Of course not. Why?"

"Because I actually know you. You're the one who used to take notes on back-to-school night."

Big is still drinking coffee and reading the paper when Leda returns home. "How did your interview go?"

"Terrible. My source withdrew."

"You need to be tougher, Mom. Ask the hard-hitting questions, like Dad. You should watch Meet the Press for inspiration."

"Is Little up yet?"

"Yeah. He went out."

"Where?" She wishes she hadn't insisted, when they were younger, that they not tattle on each other.

Big rolls his eyes. "Library." This is a ruse from middle school. At the library, you're supposed to turn off your cell phone. Your parents can't reach you.

"I hope he realizes how early your flight is tomorrow. We need to leave the house at six a.m."

"He realizes," Big says. "Little's in college now. You need to stop worrying about him."

Since he was about four years old, Big has considered himself Leda's peer advisor. Thirty years from now, she figures, he'll be taking charge of her checkbook, hiding her car keys from her.

"Do you remember a guy from the Sun, sandy-haired, sort of pudgy?" Leda asks Joe later that night.

"I can think of ten people like that," Joe says. "Drinks too much?"

"Probably."

"Now I can think of twenty. Why?"

"He told me that when I went to Boston to do the poetry program you became a workaholic."

"That almost makes it sound like a bad thing." Joe takes off his shoes and socks. They both look at his white, white feet, with red marks from his laces.

"Were you really traumatized when I left?" Leda says. "You never asked me to stay." Nine months later, though, he'd called and asked her to marry him.

"Wait," Joe says. "He said I talked about being traumatized in the newsroom? That's bullshit. If I said anything, which is doubtful, I was bragging about you. It was the eighties--nobody was quitting their jobs to write poetry. And you published that poem."

"I published that poem."

"Who is this clown, anyway?"

"A source for my book. I've promised everyone anonymity, remember."

"Remind me why I encouraged you to interview a bunch of strangers about their sex lives," Joe says. He takes off his pants, shirt and tie, thumps his own belly. "I'm taking care of this, Leda. And I'm going to start showering twice a day. Don't you fret. We'll get it back, my love."

She's laughing now, so hard she has to sit down.

He goes into the bathroom and turns on the shower.

She checks her phone, and there's still no message from Little. She'll ask Joe if he's heard from him. She opens the bathroom door, and when it sticks, gives it a hard shove.

"Ow! Jesus!" Joe is lying on the bathroom rug, facedown in a pool of blood. The shower is still running, steaming up the room.

She kneels at his side. He puts a hand to his temple, and stares at the blood covering his fingertips. "Jesus."

"Don't move, Joe. Do you remember falling? Are you numb anywhere?"

He makes an impatient noise. "Of course I remember falling. I was doing push-ups and you whacked me with the edge of the door." He sits up, and blood is still coming from the gash. "Get a towel. I think I need stitches."

She fetches a pair of sweats from Big's bedroom floor. Even those aren't easy to get on him, since he refuses to take his hands from the towel pressed to his head, but he can hardly go to the emergency room naked.

She hasn't told Joe about the statistic she found during her research, that thirty percent of men who have heart attacks have them during sex. Do their partners try to make them decent before the ambulance arrives? It had seemed a black joke, Nelson Rockefeller dying in the arms of a mistress, but actually it's a leading national tragedy. Sex, it turns out, cannot be made safe.

Both boys are still out but the car, luckily, is in the driveway; and luckily, two nights after New Year's Eve is a slow time at the hospital. Joe and Leda are whisked right in. "Without a reservation," Joe murmurs. He's increasingly cheerful as the Percocet and Lidocaine kick in. "I don't feel a thing," he announces gaily, three or four times, as the doctor sews him up. Leda grips his hand anyway. Eight stitches. A line goes right up the side of his temple. "You'll only look like Frankenstein for a couple of weeks until the stitches come out," the doctor says.

"You know, the monster wasn't Frankenstein," Joe says. "That was the doctor's name."

Leda is asked to step out of the room. What could they be doing to Joe more gruesome than what she's just witnessed? She checks her phone, and there's still no message from Little. She leaves a voicemail for him; another for Big, who texts back: I'm home, and yes, Mom, I'm packing.

A woman in surgical scrubs walks by. She looks familiar, with long-lashed, dark eyes. A Dr. Shah is paged, and the woman picks up her pace. Why, she must be Liban's mother--maybe she knows if the boys are together. Leda follows the retreating blue figure down a corridor, through a set of rubber-framed swinging doors. She'd always intended to invite this woman to coffee--why didn't she? Life is so brief, so fragile...a sob catches in her throat. Hospitals always make one so emotional.

An orderly approaches her. "Can I help you?"

"I just saw someone I think I know."

"This isn't a shopping mall, ma'am. Please go back the way you came."

Joe gets his discharge papers and a tiny manila envelope with more Percocet. In the car, he tells her that when she left the room he was asked if anything had happened that evening that he was afraid to mention in front of her.

"I'm glad to hear that," Leda says. "I mean I'm glad there's gender parity about domestic violence."

"I mentioned the chicken in peanut sauce we had for dinner. The doctor was sympathetic."

"You didn't like the chicken?"

"Something about the peanut butter. It keeps repeating. I'm sorry."

She grips the steering wheel. The streetlights blur and acquire halos. She's going to cry again. She pulls over. "Joe, where in God's name is Little?"

"What do you mean?"

"He hasn't been seen since this morning."

"Seen by whom?"

"By anyone. I've called and texted him and he doesn't answer. He and Big are supposed to catch their flight in four hours."

"Where's Big?"

"He's home. He apparently doesn't know where Little is."

"I'm sure he's home by now."

But he isn't.

They wake Big. "Do you mind, guys? I have to get up early tomorrow." He blinks and stares at Joe. "Don't freak out, Dad, but there's like a centipede on your forehead."

"They're stitches," Joe says. "Mom hit me."

"Joe!"

"Domestic violence isn't a joking matter," Big says reprovingly.

"I left you a huge long message from the hospital," Leda says. "Didn't you get it?"

"Nobody my age listens to their voicemail, Mom."

"Well, listen to this: you've got to tell us where your brother is."

"But I don't know."

"I saw blood coming out of his mouth last night," Leda says.

"You must have been dreaming," Joe says.

"I wasn't dreaming," Leda says, though now she feels uncertain. Why didn't she question Little, instead of drifting back to bed?

"It wasn't a dream," Big says. "Do you know Grace?"

"Grace? What does Grace have to do with it?"

"What do you mean by grace, exactly?" Joe says woozily. He ought to be in bed.

"All I know is that a girl named Grace gave a New Year's Eve party," Leda says.

"She showed up at our house last night," Big says. "Little was blown away. He didn't think she even knew who he was, much less where he lives."

"But Little said he knew her really well."

Big laughs, not unkindly. "Grace? Uh-uh."

"Is she a celebrity?"

"In a way. All the guys know who she is. Don't make that face, Mom. I mean that she's extremely pretty. Anyway, she showed up, and Little was stunned."

"Did he get in a fight over her?"

Big looks exasperated. "Little? Can you picture Little slugging it out over a woman?"

"I suppose not." Though Leda's mental picture of Little is all wrong, anyhow. She still walks by toy store windows and sees stuffed animals he would love.

"So we were just chilling on the porch when Little decides he has to have a bowl of raisin bran. And Grace starts singing and pretending Little's cereal bowl is a wishing well, and she throws a penny in it."

"She could have killed him!" Leda cries, indignant.

"OK, but at the time, it was funny. She thought Little saw it, but he was looking at her, and we're outside so it's dark. He gets the penny on his spoon and bites down and breaks his molar. It's bleeding like crazy, and Grace is crying, and everything's messed up. If we were allowed to smoke weed in the house, this never would have happened, is what I'm saying."

"No," Joe says sharply. Suddenly he seems to shake off his painkillers, like a dog shaking off water. He takes out his phone. "First we need to find Grace, because she may know where Little is. What's her last name?"

"I have no idea," Big says. "She didn't go to our school."

"She lives just a few streets over," Leda says. "We can go there and knock on doors." She meets Joe's eyes. They know how to track people down, how to ask the hard-hitting questions. They are colleagues and getting answers is their religion.

"At three in the morning?" Big says. "That's insane."

"You have no idea," Leda says.

"Wait," Big says. He sighs. "Little is in New York. OK, not New York any more--they were just north of Baltimore last I talked to him. They should be here soon. I wasn't lying when I said I didn't know where he was. His phone was running out of juice, and he didn't want to wake Grace. She drove him there to get his tooth fixed, because she has a brother in Hoboken who's a dentist or in dental school or something. But Little made me promise not to tell you unless the situation got desperate because he was afraid you and Dad would think it was a stupid thing to do."

"He's right," Joe says finally. He collapses heavily on the edge of the bed. "It was a really stupid thing to do."

Leda can't speak. Relief is washing over her. It's making an actual sound, a rushing in her ears. Someday, disaster will strike one of them--all of them--she knows that. But, for one day more, the force field of her worry has held fate at bay.

Big flops back down on the pillow. He's snoring before the light is out.

"Don't you want to have a nap?" Joe says to her. "I'll set the alarm for five--that'll get us to the airport on time."

She shakes her head--she's too happy and relieved to sleep. She goes into Little's room, though there's nothing for her to do here: his suitcases are packed. She turns off the light and sits at the window. It's four o'clock and the sky is black but for a few stars, glittering like bits of broken glass. The neighborhood is silent, undisturbed by her frantic knocking.

In Mexico, the roosters would begin crowing at this hour, and smoke would curl from the cooking fires. Then the feral dogs would start howling, and there'd be the anguished squeals of a neighborhood pig who somehow understood it was his day to go to market. Sunlight would flood over the rim of Popocatepetl, as if the entire mountain were bursting into flame.

Daybreak would invariably send Little into deep, contented slumber--satisfied that his nightly vigil had once again made the sun rise.

Leda rests her head on her arms and closes her eyes. The windowsill rocks gently. She sees Little sailing home along the Baltimore-Washington parkway, the music booming as the sky lightens, glancing now and then at the pearly face of the girl sleeping beside him, beaming to himself at his amazing powers, his amazing good luck.

Contributor's Notes

Ned Balbo's third book, *The Trials of Edgar Poe and Other Poems* (Story Line Press), was awarded the 2010 Donald Justice Prize and the 2012 Poets' Prize. *Lives of the Sleepers* (U. of Notre Dame Press), received the Ernest Sandeen Prize and a *ForeWord* Book of the Year Gold Medal; *Galileo's Banquet* (WWPH) shared the Towson University Prize. A selection of poems based on the paintings of Nora Sturges appears in the 2012 *Avatar Review*, and variations on poems by Apollinaire, Baudelaire, Rilke, Rimbaud, Trakl, and Valéry are out or forthcoming in *Able Muse, Bluestem, Evansville Review, String Poet, Unsplendid,* and elsewhere. He is co-winner of the 2013 Willis Barnstone Translation Prize.

Destiny Birdsong is currently a lecturer and academic adviser at Vanderbilt University, where she received her MFA in poetry in 2009, and her Ph.D. in English in 2012. Her work has appeared in *RATTLE, Tidal Basin Review, Cave Canem Anthology XII: Poems (2008-2009), Handful of Dust,* and other publications.

Jude Brancheau teaches English composition at Ming Chuan University in Taipei, Taiwan. He received his MA in English from Miami University and his poems have appeared or are forthcoming in *Southern Poetry Review, Cold Mountain Review, Indiana Review, The Florida Review,* and the *North American Review*.

Janet Buttenwieser's nonfiction work has appeared several places, including *Bellevue Literary Review, Los Angeles Review,* and *Cirque,* and won honorable mention in *The Atlantic* 2010 Student Writing contest. She has an MFA from the Whidbey Writers Workshop.

Joseph Cassara is a graduate of Columbia University. His work has been published in the *Asymptote Journal* and *PANK*, among others. He writes and teaches in Barcelona.

Ekaterina Chapiro is fluent in three languages and devotes much of her time to poetry writing and translating. She studies English and Russian philology at Copenhagen University, and has worked with translation for several years. She is of Russian origin, received all of her education in English, and resides in Denmark.

Noel Crook's book, *Salt Moon*, winner of the 2013 Crab Orchard Review First Book Award, will be published in early 2015 by Southern Illinois University Press. Her chapbook, *Canyon*, was published by Red Dragonfly Press in 2010 and her poems have appeared in *The Atlanta Review, New Letters, Shenandoah, Smartish Pace* and other journals. She is a graduate of the MFA Program in Creative Writing at North Carolina State University.

Holly Day is a mother of two living in Minnesota. Her poetry has recently appeared in *Hawaii Pacific Review, Slant,* and *The Tampa Review,* and she is the 2011 recipient of the Sam Ragan Poetry Prize from Barton College.

George Dila is the author of a short story collection, *Nothing More to Tell,* published by Mayapple Press in 2011. His short fiction and personal essays have appeared in numerous journals, including *North American Review, Cleaver, Palooka, Literal Latte, Fiction Now, Pithead Chapel* and others.

Kaitlin Dyer is a founding editor of *Harlot: A Revealing Look at the Arts of Persuasion.* Her work has appeared in *PANK, Poetry International, Web del Sol,* and *Hawaii Pacific Review.* She lives in Buenos Aires, Argentina.

Nausheen Eusuf is a Ph.D. student in English at Boston University. She holds an MA from the Writing Seminars at Johns Hopkins, and her poems have appeared in *Agenda, Mezzo Cammin, Spillway, Louisville Review,* and other journals. Her chapbook *What Remains* was published by Longleaf Press at Methodist University.

Kristin N. Faatz is a writer and pianist. She studied engineering and music at Swarthmore College, piano performance at the Peabody Institute, and fiction writing at the Johns Hopkins University. Her short fiction has appeared in *Umbrella Factory Magazine* (Sept 2012) and *The Kenyon Review's* KROnline (fall 2013). Her first novel, *Four-Hands,* draws on her experience of the behind-the-scenes world of the classical symphony. Ms. Faatz is an active studio teacher and performing artist in Maryland.

Corey Ginsberg's work has most recently appeared in such publications as *PANK, the Cream City Review, Memoir(and), Third Coast,* and the *Nashville Review,* among others. Corey currently lives in Florida and works as a freelance writer.

Eileen Gonzalez is a graduate student at Johns Hopkins University, where she studies digital communication. Her debut novel, tentatively titled *A Nice Wardrobe,* will be available on the Kindle later this year. She is on Twitter @EileenDGonzalez

David Goodrich is a retired climate scientist. An avid bicyclist, he has ridden from Delaware to Oregon, down the Appalachians, and on the Way of St. James in Spain.

Paul Grams earned degrees in Linguistics and English Literature; he taught in the Detroit Public Schools, mostly grades 6-9, for 30 years; he ran scholastic chess programs there. He's retired to Maryland. Two books of his poems have been published.

Kathleen Gunton believes one art feeds another. She is committed to literary publications. Her photography and poems often appear in the same journal. Recent images in *Arts & Letters, Broad River Review, Owen Wister Review, Perceptions, Raven Chronicles, Thema,* and *Switchback.* She lives in California.

Jeff Hardin is the author of two collections, *Fall Sanctuary* and *Notes for a Praise Book.* His third collection, *Restoring the Narrative,* recently received the Donald Justice Poetry Prize and will appear in 2015. His work can be found in recent issues of *Unsplendid, Southern Review, North American Review, The Laurel Review, Missouri Review (online), New Orleans Review,* and elsewhere.

Peleg Held was a former member of Voices in the Wilderness. He is a carpenter in Maine.

Ryan Hibbett is an English instructor at Northern Illinois University, specializing in twentieth-century British poetry. His articles have appeared in *Twentieth-Century Literature* and *Contemporary Literature,* and he has published poetry in *Atlanta Review, Mad Poets Review,* and *Sierra Nevada Review.*

Amy Holman is the author of *Wrens Fly Through This Opened Window* and the prizewinning *Wait For Me, I'm Gone,* as well as a writer's guide to colonies, residencies, grad programs, and grants. This is her second appearance in *The Potomac Review.* She is a literary consultant in New York.

Jane Hoogestraat's book of poems *Border States* won the 2013 John Ciardi Prize and will be published by BkMk Press in 2014. In addition, she has published in such journals as *Elder Mountain, Fourth River, Image, Midwestern Gothic, Poetry,* and *Southern Review*. She teaches at Missouri State.

Beth Konkoski is a writer and high school English teacher. She lives with her husband and two children in Northern Virginia. Her fiction has appeared in *Story, Mid-American Review,* and *Gargoyle*. Her poetry chapbook, *Noticing the Splash* is available from BoneWorld Press.

Rachel Kubie is a public reference librarian in Charlotte, NC. She attended the Writing Seminars at Johns Hopkins and has an MLS from Catholic University in DC. Her poems have appeared or are upcoming in *Mudlark, Drunken Boat, Literal Latte, Rattapallax,* and *Sou'wester*. She recently took part in the *Tupelo Press* 30/30 project online, and has had poems in the anthologies *Imperial Messages: 100 Modern Parables (2nd ed.)* and *Final Harvest: Jewish Writing From St. Louis*.

Gerry LaFemina is the author of numerous books of poetry and fiction including 2013's *Notes for the Novice Ventriloquist* (Mayapple Press, prose poems) and *Clamor* (Codorus Press, novel) and the forthcoming *Little Heretic* (Stephen F Austin University Press, poems). He directs the Center for Creative Writing at Frostburg State University where he is an Associate Professor of English.

Martin H. Levinson is a member of the Authors Guild, National Book Critics Circle, and is the book review editor for *ETC: A Review of General Semantics*. He has published 8 books and numerous articles and poems in various publications. He holds a Ph.D. from NYU and lives in New York.

Peter Makuck's *Long Lens: New & Selected Poems* was published in 2010 by BOA Editions, Ltd. and nominated for a Pulitzer Prize. His third collection of short stories, *Allegiance and Betrayal*, was released last year by Syracuse University Press. His work has appeared in *The Hudson Review, Poetry, The Sewanee Review,* and *Yale Review.*

William Miller is a widely published poet and children's author. His poems have appeared in *The Southern Review, Shenandoah,* and *Prairie Schooner.* He lives in New Orleans.

Dan Moreau lives in Northern California.

Kathleen O'Toole has combined a professional life in community organizing with teaching and writing. Her poetry has appeared widely in journals including *Poetry, America, Little Patuxent Review, Margie, Poetry East,* and *Prairie Schooner.* A chapbook *Practice* was published in 2005, and *Meanwhile,* her first full-length collection, in 2011.

Eric Reymond is a lector in Biblical Hebrew at Yale Divinity School. His professional research concerns ancient poetry and literary expression, especially in ancient Semitic languages like Ugaritic, Hebrew, and Aramaic. His creative work has appeared, among other places, in *Denver Quarterly* and *New Orleans Review.*

Paige Riehl's poetry has been published in *Meridian, South Dakota Review, Nimrod,* and more. She won the 2012-2013 Loft Mentor Series in Poetry and the 2011 *Literal Latte* Prize for Poetry. She was a semi-finalist for the 2011 Pablo Neruda Prize for Poetry and the 2011 *River Styx* International Poetry Contest.

Jane Satterfield's most recent book is *Her Familiars* (Elixir, 2013). She is the author of two previous poetry collections: *Assignation* *at Vanishing Point*, and *Shepherdess with an Automatic*, as well as *Daughters of Empire: A Memoir of a Year in Britain and Beyond*. Her awards include a National Endowment for the Arts Fellowship in poetry, the William Faulkner Society's Gold Medal for the Essay, the *Florida Review* Editors' Prize in nonfiction, and the *Mslexia* women's poetry prize. In 2013, she was awarded the 49th Parallel Poetry Prize from *The Bellingham Review* for her poem "Elegy with Trench Art and Asanas."

Mikhail Konstantinovich Scherbakov is a prominent Russian poet, songwriter and bard. Since 1978, he has been consistently active with numerous album releases and live performances. He graduated from Moscow State University's Faculty of Philology in 1988, and now lives in Moscow.

Wendy Scott's book, *Soon I Will Build an Ark*, will be published in 2014 by Main Street Rag. Her poems have appeared or are forthcoming in *Paterson Literary Review, Fourth River, Cobalt Review, Punchnel's*, and the *Pittsburgh City Paper*, among others. She has an MFA from the University of Pittsburgh.

Peter Serchuk's poems have appeared in a variety of journals including *Boulevard, Poetry, New Letters, North American Review, Texas Review* and others. His work has also been featured on Garrison Keillor's *The Writer's Almanac*. He is the author of two collections: *Waiting for Poppa at the Smithtown Diner* (University of Illinois Press) and most recently, *All That Remains* (WordTech Editions 2012). He lives in California.

Leona Sevick is Associate Provost and Associate Professor of English at Mount St. Mary's University. She earned her doctorate in English at the University of Maryland. Her recent work appears in *Barrow Street, the Delaware Poetry Review*, and

Naugatuck River Review. She is winner of the 2012 Split this Rock Poetry Contest, judged by Naomi Shihab Nye.

Spencer Smith is a University of Utah graduate and works in the corporate world to pay the bills that poetry doesn't pay (i.e. all of them). His poetry has appeared in over thirty literary journals. Besides writing, he enjoys a variety of literature and music, and spending time with family.

Peter P. Sordillo is a physician and cancer researcher, who also has graduate degrees in philosophy and physics. He frequently writes on scientific and philosophical topics. His poetry has appeared in *The Iowa Review, Connecticut Review,* and *Bellevue Literary Review.* He lives in New York with his wife and children.

Dario Sulzman received his MFA in Creative Writing from Florida State University. His work has appeared previously in *Gulfstream, Apt Magazine,* and *The Massachusetts Review.* He currently lives in Ohio, where he attends the University of Cincinnati as a doctoral candidate in Creative Writing.

Kelly M. Sylvester's highlights include contributing poetry reviews for NewPages.com, publications in various literary magazines. She received the 2006 Bernard Grebanier Best Sonnet Award and also Beatrice Dubin Rose Poetry Award honorable mention. Her creative thesis, *Learning Content through Poetry Writing,* produced *Alva: A Collection of Poetry.* She was the 2013 Millersville University's Graduate Commencement Moment of Reflection Speaker. She holds two Master of Education degrees.

Savannah Thorne graduated from the University of Iowa and her poetry has appeared in nearly two dozen literary journals, including *Potpourri, Yemassee, Parabola,* and *The Atlanta Review.* She recently became managing editor for *Conclave: A Journal of*

Character, and her historical novel is represented by Trident Media Group.

Tina Tocco's work has appeared in *Harpur Palate, Passages North, Italian Americana, Clockhouse Review, Inkwell, Border Crossing,* and *The Westchester Review,* among other publications. She was a finalist in *CALYX*'s 2013 Flash Fiction Contest for "Promised Land" and "21 Days". Tina earned her MFA in creative writing from Manhattanville College, where she was editor-in-chief of *Inkwell*.

LaToya Watkins is a Ph.D. candidate at the University of Texas at Dallas. Her stories have appeared in numerous online and print publications, including *Specter, Lunch Ticket: Antioch, Los Angeles, Kweli Journal,* and *Ruminate Magazine*. She resides in Texas with her family.

Colleen Wells writes from Indiana, where she lives with her husband and three children. Her work has appeared in *Adoptive Families Magazine* and *The Georgetown Review*. She has an MFA from Spalding University. She works in education and aspires to go into human services focusing on mental health.

Kathleen Wheaton grew up in California and lived subsequently in Madrid, Boston, New York, Buenos Aires, Rio de Janeiro and Tepoztlan, Mexico. Her collection, *Aliens and Other Stories,* won the 2013 Washington Writers Publishing House Fiction Prize. She works as a freelance magazine writer and Spanish and Portuguese interpreter. She currently lives in Maryland.